BOOKS BY C.B. WILSON

Jack Russelled to Death

Cavaliered to Death

Bichoned to Death

Shepherded to Death

Doodled to Death

Corgied to Death

Aussied to Death (Coming Summer 2023)

CORGIED TO DEATH

C.B. WILSON

For Rocky
My Happily Ever After

Dolphin Training Center

Fishtails Seaside Cafe

1. Bow Wow Boutique
2. Posh Puppies
3. Bichon Bisquets
4. Beg-als Shoppe
5. Muttropolis
6. Woofing Best Coffe

7. Urban Pup
8. Snooty Pooch
9. Fluff & Buff
10. Fiesta Chihuahua

11. Bank
12. Gem's Palace
13. Blooming Tails
14. Taj Ma Hound

Cat's Town House

Homes

Oldman home
(circa 1900-1925)

Red Door Speakeasy
(circa 1920-1925)

K9 Fine Wine Bar

Sea Dog Scuba Shop

Hounds Hardware

Graveyard & Ghost

Frosty Pup

15. Hot Dog Stand
16. Bone Garden Salad
17. Attorney
18. Escrow
19. Hair Salon

Chateau Chien

Salty Dog Seafood

Doodle Pad

Mutt Hutt

Dogwood

KDOG Studio

A Lifeguard Tower

Bark Rock

Dolce

Kanine

Ciao Bella

Dog House

B Old Barkview Inn

WOOF

Smy

DOG PATH

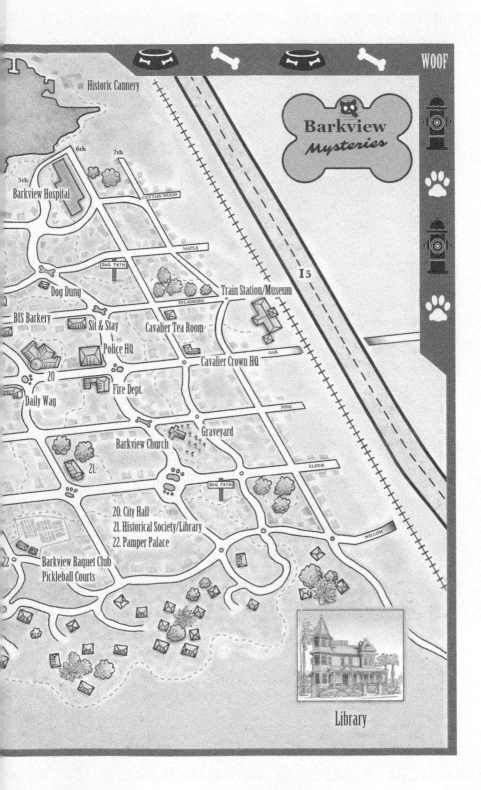

WOOF

Historic Cannery

Barkview
Mysteries

6th
7th
5th
Barkview Hospital
COTTON WOOD
MAPLE
DOG PATH
I 5
Dog Dung
SYCAMORE
Train Station/Museum
BIS Barkery
Sit & Stay
Cavalier Tea Room
Police HQ
Cavalier Crown HQ
OAK
20
Fire Dept.
Daily Wag
PINE
Graveyard
Barkview Church
ELDER
21.
DOG PATH
20. City Hall
21. Historical Society/Library
22. Pamper Palace
WILLOW
22
Barkview Raquet Club
Pickleball Courts

Library

CHARACTERS, HUMAN

Barklay, Celeste: Founder of Barkview in 1890.

Barklay, Charlotte (Aunt Char): Mayor of Barkview, dog psychiatrist on *Throw Him a Bone*. Renny, a champion Cavalier King Charles Spaniel, is her dog.

Barklay, JB: Aunt Char's late husband.

Douglas, Jonathan: Rumrunner lost in 1925. Owner of the Douglas Diamond. Married to Marie.

Gibbs, Chris: Forensic Pathologist.

Hana: Political consultant.

Hawl, Russ: Cat's fiancé. FBI consultant. Owns Blue Diamond Security.

James, Jesse: Barkview Bank manager. Brutus & Caesar, Bull-mastiffs, are his dogs.

Jones, Henry: Spy operating in Barkview in 1940's

Moore, Jennifer: Librarian. Nutmeg & Cinnamon are her dogs

Ohana, Lani: Cat's half-sister.

Ohana, Mary Ann: Cat's mother.

Oldeman, Will: Old Barkview Inn elevator operator

Oldeman, William Sr.: Will's grandfather.

Madame Orr: Barkview's fortune-teller/psychic. Danior, a Bedlington Terrier, is her dog.

Papas, Ariana: Owner of Gem's Palace Jewelry. Gem, a German Shepherd, is Ariana's dog.

Powell, Paula (Pawprints): Centurion protector of Barkview. CJ's Mother. Married to Charles Smythe. Winston is her dog.

Roma, Victor, Jr.: Chairman of Firebird Industries.

Schmidt, Gregory (Uncle G): Barkview's police chief. Max and Maxine, silver-point German Shepherds, are his dogs.

Smythe, Adam: Former mayor of Barkview.

Smythe, Charles: Adam Smythe's Great Uncle.

Smythe, CJ: Paula and Charles' son.

Smythe Chelsea: Adam's daughter. Lady Mag is her dog.

Tanaka, Hiro: Japanese American lived in Barkview in 1940's

Tanaka, Miyo: Hiro's daughter. Lotus is her dog.

Thompson, Jordan: Owner of the Sea Dog Dive Shop.

Turner, Gabby: Owner of the Daily Wag Coffee Bar. Sal, a Saluki, is her dog.

Williams, Chad: Treasure hunter searching for the Douglas Diamond.

Wright, Catalina "Cat": Producer/investigative reporter at KDOG. A cat person living in Barkview.

Wynne, Sandy: Cat's assistant and computer whiz. Jack, a Jack Russell Terrier, is her dog.

Yamaguchi, Michael: Owner Kanine Karate.

Yamaguchi, Hurato: Michael's Uncle killed in 1942.

CHARACTERS, CANINE

🐾 Cinnamon & Nutmeg: Jennifer Moore's Cavalier King Charles Spaniels.

🐾 Brutus & Caesar: Jesse James' Bullmastiffs.

🐾 Danior: Madame Orr's Bedlington Terrier.

🐾 Gem: Ariana's German Shepherd.

🐾 Jack: Sandy's Jack Russell Terrier.

🐾 Lady Mag: Chelsea Smythe's Cavalier King Charles

🐾 Lotus: Miyo Tanaka's Shiba Inu

🐾 Max and Maxine: Uncle G's German Shepherds.

🐾 Renny: Aunt Char's champion Cavalier King Charles Spaniel.

🐾 Sal: Gabby's Saluki dog

🐾 Winston: Paula (Pawprints) Powell's Corgi

CHAPTER 1

~~Dogfight in Barkview. Bow wow battle cry~~. I scratched out yet another headline. The stress had to be getting to me. Or was my creativity just buried somewhere in that leaning tower of must-do paperwork on my executive desk?

My name is Catalina Wright, Cat to my friends. I have one of those dream jobs coveted by leash lovers everywhere. I produce, manage, and write content for KDOG, the premier TV station in Barkview, the dog-friendliest city in America. I kid you not. Here, leash lanes lead to hound playgrounds, and every resident has a BFF. That's a Best Furry Friend. Except me.

I don't hate dogs. In fact, after my previous five fido adventures, I've come to value a number of canine qualities. I simply prefer sleek, independent, and litter box–trained cats, which makes me the most unpopular person in town. That is, until my Aunt Char, Barkview's mayor and the quintessential voice of congeniality, got territorial and turned last night's City Council meeting dog-eat-dog.

Sandy Wynne, my perky, voice of the millennials assistant, rushed into my office. She tucked a flyaway strand of long blonde hair behind her ear and waved her tablet as if it were a weapon. Like me, she'd dressed in black slacks and a striped blouse. Jack, her hyperactive Jack Russell Terrier, *grrr*'d at her feet. "Paula is dead."

As if on cue, the morning briefing pinged on my computer screen, confirming everything.

Paula "Paw Prints" Powell Dead at a Hundred and One

No way! Just last night, the woman had stormed out of the council meeting, brandishing her Corgi-headed walking stick. Her parting words: "You pursue digging up the past over my dead body, Charlotte Barklay." Paula's blazing blue gaze had then locked with mine, double-dog daring me to defy her.

Talk about a waving flag. Uncovering secrets drove me— the bigger, the better. Everyone knew it. Blame it on the investigative reporter in me demanding answers—answers, I hated to admit, that oftentimes were better left buried. In this case, answers to a historic find dating back to the 1940s.

"It makes no sense that Paula opposed honoring the accomplishments of World War II radio interceptors." I jerked my fingers through my shoulder-length tawny mane. In this old town full of Victorian homes, remodels often unearthed significant past events. My aunt had been elected mayor on her promise to celebrate our community's extraordinary contributions to history.

"This must be something big for Paula to take such a hard stand." Sandy's ominous comment hung over us like the typical California-morning coastal clouds.

No kidding. When your town's oldest living citizen and a true icon demands that you "stay away" from something, do you just blindly agree? Paula had seen and done so much for Barkview. In fact, a bronze statue depicting her dressed in overalls and her slouchy, outback hat with her faithful Corgi at her heels presided over Bark Park, where she'd been protecting our shores for the past eighty years. Japanese invaders, drug smugglers, or rogue sharks—nothing got by her.

Curiosity still tugged at me. "Why blindside my aunt? The meeting's agenda has been public all week. Paula could've just voiced her concerns. Aunt Char's door is always open."

"Her dramatic display bothered me too," Sandy admitted. "I'm shocked Paula chose to rile everyone up."

I wasn't. I'd interviewed Paula for the launch of her granddaughter's book documenting Paula's World War II dog patrol contributions. She'd hinted at a secret she intended to reveal in due time. After several months of useless poking around, I'd written off her stories to eccentricity. She certainly had her fair share of it.

"Why did Mrs. B vote to continue the information-gathering process anyway?" No matter her political title, my aunt would always be Mrs. B, the supportive parent figure Sandy had admired when she'd arrived in Barkview a couple of years ago.

"Paula's refusal to explain her position made matters worse," I added.

"Paula can—could be stubborn," Sandy admitted. "But usually she was right."

The same could be said about Aunt Char. I took a calming breath. Paula's passing wasn't the end of this controversy. I could feel it. "Anything suspicious about Paula's death?" I hoped not. The woman was ancient.

"Our police sources indicated a standard information lockdown pending notification of next of kin. Paula's granddaughter is on a book tour someplace in Europe right now," Sandy replied.

Nothing odd about that, but my intuition still twinged.

Sandy saw it too. Jack's bark did not completely block out her groan. "Rumor has it your aunt went to Paula's house last night." Sandy referred to her tablet. "Three sightings confirm her entering Paula's driveway at 9:15 p.m."

Who needed social media when Barkview's gossip super-highway worked so well? My dread notched up. "What else are the gossips saying?" I asked, but I already knew.

"That your aunt killed her." Sandy flopped into my less-than-comfortable straight- backed visitor's chair. Although I'd decorated my office to pay tribute to the two-level Victorian's storied past with warm cherry wood furnishings and wall-to-wall bookcases, I'd intentionally chosen the stiff chairs to discourage inquisitive newsies from hanging out.

My protective instincts kicked in. "That's insane. We don't even know what caused her death."

"Let's hope it was old age," Sandy said.

My phone dinged with a text from the police chief. Real fear stirred. I read the message twice before speaking. "Pack your camera. Our presence is requested at Paula's house."

Sandy's gape summed up my feelings exactly. Although I called the chief of police "Uncle," he was not a true blood relative, but rather my Aunt Char's second husband's brother-in-law. Not that the pet name helped me any. My citations could finance the annual police puppy parade. Only in Barkview could failure to yield the sidewalk to an oncoming Pekinese be a finable offense.

Since Uncle G generally shunned the press, this invitation couldn't be good news, nor was it an at-your-convenience request. Sandy hurriedly enlisted a dog-sitter for her Jack Russell and gathered her camera gear. Eleven minutes later, she sat beside me in my Jag SUV as I turned onto First Street. I followed the shoreline past the iconic Queen Anne–style Old Barkview Inn to the twisty-turny, tree-lined road leading to the

Terraces. Located due south of downtown, the hillside homes enjoyed expansive sunset views of the Pacific Ocean, cool breezes, and privacy not often found in Southern California. Barkview's elite resided here, the higher up the hill, the more exclusive.

I stopped at the barricade of orange cones blocking Paula's driveway. The officer moved the obstacle and waved us right through the iron gates. Inside, two police SUVs and a familiar white Tesla filled the circular driveway in front of a mid-century modern home.

Once a prominent dog-training kennel, the home featured a thriving cottage garden and coastal live oaks separating the Craftsman-style outbuildings from the sprawling main structure. The sweeping ocean view included Bark Rock, which made lounging on the porch swing idyllic.

That KDOG's well-dressed lawyer, Mark Wilton, met us on the rose-trellised porch didn't bode well at all. "Is Aunt Char in trouble?" My heart rabbit-raced. Why else would he be here?

Mark straightened his wire-rimmed glasses. "No. Nothing like that. I was Paula's estate lawyer. I am here to deliver this at her request." He handed me a bulging manila envelope. "She left instructions for you in her office."

No doubt why Uncle G had summoned me. My fingers itched to rip the paper open and discover the contents. I squeezed the envelope. The bulge felt hard, like a book—a diary, maybe. What could Paula possibly want to give me? "When did she give this to you?"

"A few months ago." Mark motioned toward my car. "I suggest you put the envelope out of sight before you go inside."

Good plan. I dropped it in my back seat and made it back to the porch just as Uncle G's arrival ended further conversation.

"Come see me if you have additional questions." Mark departed with a wave.

Flanked by Max and Maxine, the iron-gray German Shepherds that matched his neatly clipped Santa beard and full head of hair, the chief of police proved my theory that masters choose physically similar canine companions. The silver epaulets on his blue shirt even coordinated with the dogs' police vests.

The German Shepherds' attack-ready stances sent awareness through the scar beneath my signature neck scarf. My rational mind knew these well-trained dogs weren't going to bite me without reason, but once-bit-forever-on-guard certainly applied to me in regard to any big dog. "I take it this isn't a social call."

An answering bark from deep inside the house drew my attention. I'd forgotten about Paula's faithful fawn-colored Pembroke Corgi.

Uncle G pointed at Sandy. "Camera stays at the door, and no specifics."

"Got it." This visit was off the record.

At my nod, the chief motioned us to put on blue booties and follow, his signature toothpick spinning between his lips.

I paused, my intuition suddenly on high alert. I sensed danger in this well-lived-in home overflowing with fragrant red-tipped yellow roses and worn throw rugs.

Armed police officers guarding the entrance didn't alleviate my trepidation or still my runaway imagination. Something had happened here. I knew it.

I matched Uncle G's long strides step-for-step until we arrived at a tightly closed ornate double door. I doubted the officer with neon orange peeking out of his ears heard Uncle G's command, but he stepped aside anyway. The chief walked right in.

Sandy and I followed slightly more cautiously. Decorated in a charming, shabby-chic cottage style, the room's twin floral-printed wing-back chairs faced floor-to-ceiling book-cases. My heart rate spiked the moment I saw Paula's Corgi, Winston, sitting dead center on top of the heavy mahogany executive desk.

The oddness struck me first. "How did he get up...?" The dog's high-pitched bark cut off my question.

Uncle G's booming "Quiet" did nothing. Nor did the deputy German Shepherds' puffed chests. The Corgi barked on and on. The officer's earplugs made perfect sense now. My head felt ready to explode.

"Come over here, Cat." Uncle G's finger gesture drew me closer.

I saw it then, right beneath the Corgi's fluffy butt, the standard white legal envelope Mark had mentioned. The words "To be opened by Catalina Wright" were written in Paula's distinctive, albeit shaky, script across the center.

The dog scooted aside as I approached. With a job-done shake that sent fur flying, he leaped onto the chair on his way to the ground and sat at my feet, rabbit ears up, thankfully silent.

"Care to explain?" Uncle G's brows formed a line across his forehead.

As if I had a clue. A dog owned by a woman I hardly knew had just delivered me a from-the-grave request. Where would I even start?

CHAPTER 2

The envelope felt like lead in my hands. Not that it weighed that much. The implications did. "I take it Paula didn't die from natural causes." What else could I say? I needed time to process all of this.

"Appears to be blunt force trauma to her frontal lobe," Uncle G replied.

"Could it have been an accident?" From the wooden desk to the hat stand, obstacles filled the room. Anyone could trip and fall, especially a centenarian.

"Doubtful." Uncle G crushed that glimmer of hope with a single word. "I'm waiting for the coroner's findings."

I exhaled in a rush. Not another murder investigation? The last one had about killed me. "Her walking stick?" I didn't see the distinctive Corgi-headed cane anywhere.

"Sent it to the lab."

It must have had blood on it. I gulped. "You mean she was Corgied to death?"

Not even a snicker of acknowledgment. I sobered up fast. "What was the time of death?" I dreaded his response.

"Between nine and midnight."

"You can't possibly think that Aunt Char would..." No need to feign ignorance. Never-miss-a-detail Uncle G knew my aunt's visit fit the time frame. Not again. Last time she'd been front and center in a murder investigation, I'd nearly lost her.

"Charlotte had both opportunity and motive," Uncle G said.

No fighting the opportunity. "They disagreed over a proposal," I replied.

"One of your aunt's pet projects," he shot back.

I hated it when Uncle G went devil's advocate on me. "Aunt Char wouldn't kill someone over a campaign promise. And you know it."

"What about what Paula was trying to protect?" he asked.

"Are you suggesting Paula knows something less than flattering about Aunt Char?" Good luck with that. My aunt's uncompromising moral code didn't allow for questionable behavior.

Uncle G's exhale said too much. "Every family has skeletons, including the Barklays."

"She's a Barklay by marriage. You can't seriously believe Aunt Char would kill Paula to protect the Barklay name."

"She enjoys the prominence and power the name commands. Many would like to see her come down a peg or two."

Relish was more like it. Uncle G knew the score. I suddenly got why he shunned retirement. "Petty jealousy makes me crazy. Aunt Char is..." Too many things to even verbalize. In short, my aunt epitomized all that Barkview aspired to be.

Uncle G's toothpick twirled another revolution. "I don't like this any more than you do, Cat, but I have to investigate every possible lead."

Even if it was insane. I yoga-breathed. "Maybe someone saw something. We'll open the On the Scent tip line."

"No. Panic is our enemy. Every criminal makes a mistake. I'll find it."

I had to believe that he would. "Was Aunt Char the last person to see Paula alive?"

"It appears so. I will confirm her story next. Where were you last night between nine and midnight?" Veteran military police investigative scrutiny fixed on me, questioning me better than any polygraph.

His misdirect hurt. Whose side was he on, anyway? "I went home right after the council meeting." I had. Normally, Aunt Char and I shared a coffee afterward. I drank the coffee. She preferred tea. Last night she'd canceled, clearly intending to visit Paula. I seriously needed to talk to my aunt.

"Can anyone corroborate that?" Uncle G asked.

I took great pleasure in crushing his skepticism. "I turned off my security system at nine-something." And reset it shortly thereafter. Not that it proved anything. Thanks to Barkview's no-traffic-camera policy, no one who lived alone had an airtight alibi.

Like a hound with a meaty bone, Uncle G wasn't letting go. "What's the envelope about?"

"I don't know." I almost crossed my heart. "I swear." His pointed gaze kept me talking. "Paula and I weren't best friends." We hadn't spoken at all since the interview.

"Yet she managed as her last act to leave that envelope for you," Uncle G pointed out.

"It makes no sense."

"Open it, and we both find out," Uncle G said.

More an order than a suggestion. I started to obey, but stopped. Paula had left it for my eyes only. What secrets did she want me alone to know? If this contained information

10

incriminating to Aunt Char... "I'd prefer to honor her wishes and share what she gives me permission to."

Uncle G's cough did not disguise his swear. "A woman is murdered in her home and you're withholding evidence."

"We don't know if it is relevant or not. Legally, you can't..." He could and I knew it, especially if this was a murder investigation. "Fine." I ripped open the envelope. A loose paper fluttered to the floor. No date on the note, just the same shaky script as on the envelope. I read the short note.

I apologize for the subterfuge, Cat. Although I have waited until all those personally involved have gone, some will still be hurt. It is past time to heal. You must right a great wrong perpetuated in fear. I leave you with the clues I have mulled for eighty years. Find the answers. Paula.

Uncle G's toothpick snapped with a crack. "The clues Mark Wilton delivered to you?"

No way would I get that by him. "I don't know." I did know that legally Uncle G couldn't confiscate the contents yet. "I'll look and let you know."

Uncle G's jaw tightened. "Fine. You take the dog."

"Me? No way!" Me, responsible for the chronic barker? I picked a long dog hair off my pants. Talk about terror. "When is Paula's granddaughter getting back?" The dog belonged to her.

"I'll let you know when I find her."

Which meant when I shared information, the chief would too. Ugh! Whatever was in the envelope had better be worth it. Max and Maxine's regal head tosses questioned my loyalty as they followed the chief out of the room.

11

Winston popped up to all fours, if you could call those stubby sticks legs, and wiggled his tailless fluff-butt into contortions. How weird was that? At least he wasn't barking.

Sandy laid down her camera and kneeled to scratch the dog's expressive ears. "Hey, buddy. You did good." The dog sighed in what I could only describe as pure kitty-pleasure. "I'll gather what you'll need to take him home." Before I could stop her, Sandy exited with purpose.

I shook in my kitten heels. Not that I'm paranoid, but that Corgi's cocked head intimidated me. I stood there transfixed by a pair of remarkable see-into-your-soul, cornflower-blue eyes just like Logan Roma's. The wannabe king I'd met during the Shepard Diamond heist had sworn he'd inherited those same eyes from his famous great-great-grandfather, Czar Nicholas II.

Had I come full circle? I swallowed the sudden lump in my throat. It wasn't just the color. Those blue orbs gazing straight into mine were downright arresting. I gulped. Was this a sign that the elusive Douglas Diamond that Logan still hunted would be found?

Paula had always said Winston, like his namesake, would change the world. She should know. She'd lived under Churchill and FDR's leadership and the steady stream of lesser politicians. Was she right?

Winston's barking began a good two minutes before Sandy returned carrying a bulging royal-blue duffle. I covered my ears. I'm sure my "Quiet!" command came out as a screech. The dog just shook his head and kept barking, as if I were the idiot. I had to be. At this rate I'd run away before the end of the day.

Sandy handed me earbuds. "This should help until you can work with him a little."

Teach a dog not to bark? Was that even possible? I popped

12

the headphones in. *Ah.* The soothing sound of almost silence. I suddenly got why every store in town sold them. "How did Paula tolerate all this barking?"

"She was pretty hard of hearing," Sandy replied.

"No doubt from owning generations of Corgis." Twenty, if I remembered correctly. Her neighbors had to be livid!

"You are a little oversensitive to it," Sandy remarked.

I admitted it. I'd even written an exposé on barking in Barkview. Not that it had done any good. Some dogs, I'd learned, simply had the genes for it.

"Corgis were bred to be herders. They are really smart but can be stubborn and have a lot of energy. You'll need to work with him and teach him what you expect. You'll also need to exercise him at least twice a day, and if you leave him alone you'd better give him puzzle games."

I heard her warning loud and clear. I'd just been chained to this high-maintenance dog when I had a potential murder to solve. "Wait. What? There are puzzles for dogs?"

"Yes. It's important to keep dogs like Winston focused. We'll stop at the Bow Wow Boutique on the way back to KDOG for supplies. Winston also loves to swim and paddleboard."

"That furry thing can swim?" I'd figured all that fluff to be anchor material. How could those short legs even paddle fast enough to help him float?

"It's all in the butt." Sandy chuckled. "Seriously, Corgis float because their fluffy butts are like eighty percent air. Most dogs' butts are all muscle."

That explained nothing. "He still has to hold up his head."

"And he does. Swimming is a great way to exercise him. You'll need to focus his energy."

A second warning about his energy? Not that I was a couch potato. I enjoyed a competitive pickleball game whenever possible, but hardcore running? Not in my DNA.

"How do you know all this?" Sandy tended to know everything, but this seemed extreme even for her. Unless... "Jack can stand still on a paddleboard?" Her perpetual motion terrier?

Sandy's blush confirmed my guess without words. "We're working on it. It's a great activity for us to do together."

If she didn't mind falling in the water a lot. "Is that why you want to move into my place?" No wonder she'd asked to rent my townhouse when the remodel on my new home was completed—the home my fiancé and I planned to live in after I finally chose a wedding date.

"Sort of. Jack's still a little goofy, but I have high hopes."

That dog could test even Sandy's patience-to-spare. If anyone could train that antsy, hyperactive dog to paddleboard, Sandy could. "I don't remember Winston barking this much around Paula."

"He's out of sorts. He just lost his guardian." Sandy stroked the length of his long back. "It'll be okay, Winston."

The dog rolled over to present his furry white belly. Sandy praised him and offered a treat. "Scratch him, Cat. He's trying to be friendly."

More like he wanted a belly rub, but I obeyed anyway. Fur flew in every direction. Ugh! Russ was going to sneeze his head off. Only I could be engaged to a man allergic to dogs. "How often does Winston need to be brushed?"

"I think they recommend twice a week."

"That's it?" Considering that fur explosion, I'd expected hourly.

Sandy's wry smile boded ill. "True Corgi lovers call their fur Corgi glitter."

More like an airborne hairball, based on the quantity of long fur clinging to my dark pants.

Sandy continued. "Relax. He'll shed a little. Nowhere near as bad as Jack does."

Why didn't I believe her? Her Jack Russell shed tiny needle hairs that embedded in my carpet and challenged my vacuum's deep-cleaning setting. The Corgi seemed to have a whole lot more fur.

Sandy gathered Winston in a hug. "Look how cuddly he is."

He wasn't exactly the best snuggle bear, given the way his short legs dangled down her chest and his front paws hugged her neck. I had to give him the cute face award, though. He seemed to be perpetually smiling.

"His barking is his way of talking to you," Sandy explained. "You'll need to keep him occupied and focused on you."

My confidence faltered. Low-maintenance me responsible for what sounded like a high-energy barker with a stubborn streak? I didn't need a battle of wills. I already had way too much on my plate.

"You know, you are far better suited to care for him," I suggested.

"Only if you want a roommate. My neighbors will evict me if I bring home another barking dog."

Me, live with her Jack Russell Terrier until my house was ready? Talk about motivation. One glance at Winston's alert ears and unwavering stare, and I knew I had no choice. We'd just have to figure it out together.

Much as my curiosity demanded I open the envelope screaming for attention in my back seat, I realized Corgi coexistence ranked higher. Frankly, enlisting Sandy's help now made more sense than going solo later.

I didn't cringe at the dog hair avalanche when Sandy climbed into my car with Winston on her lap. I even bit my tongue when his dusty paws left prints on the dash. The car wash could deal with it, I reminded myself, as I drove out the gates and turned left onto Ocean Drive. A visit to the Bow Wow Boutique had torture written all over it.

CHAPTER 3

Real anxiety stirred as I continued north on First Street toward the high-end dog boutique located in the north village. I passed the Old Barkview Inn on the left. Normally cloaked in the coastal low clouds, the crystal clear blue ocean drew our attention.

Sandy referred to her phone and responded before I could ask. "High pressure is building over the Four Corners. A low is off the coast. It could be a Santa Ana..."

Trust Sandy to refocus my attention. Not that I am a total fan of the so-called devil winds that brought hot, dry air from the deserts, but dared I hope? Full disclosure: Sandy and I had been hunting the long-lost Douglas Diamond for some time—along with every other treasure hunter hoping to be awarded the million-dollar finder's fee for information leading to the diamond's discovery.

After two years of research, including reading what had to have been a hundred period diaries, we were no closer to finding the treasure than anyone else. Our most promising lead remained a symbol shaped like a phoenix that reportedly could only be seen during the dust filled skies associated with a Santa Ana wind event. Needless to say, I've been not-so-patiently waiting for the easterly winds to show up.

Sandy added, "The forecast is for thirty-mile-per-hour winds. Fire danger is up."

My pulse thumped. Just maybe we'd get a chance to test our newest theory. In the meantime, I headed east on Maple and parallel parked in front of the Bow Wow Boutique. Built with the same mansard-style roof as the majority of the downtown shops, the luxury dog accessories store had a stroll-down-the-Champs-Élysées feel. As usual, Misha the Fashionista, a long-haired, silky Yorkie, met me at the door. A perpetual topper on my WDI Scale (that's my Wright Dog Insanity Scale, which rated Barkview's dog owners for over-the-top devotion to their BFFs on a scale of one to fifteen), the Yorkie lived up to my expectations. Dressed in a lace-edged pink skirt with a blingalicious vest that matched her glittering booties, she automatically rated a ten.

Winston blinked repeatedly. I'm not sure if the noon sun sparkling off the rhinestones or the insanity of it all blinded him. When Misha's owner, Alicia Bright, joined us dressed in identical attire, I quickly reassessed a WDI matchy-matchy of twelve. Only in Barkview.

"So, it's true. Paula has passed." Alicia's chocolate-colored eyes clouded.

Of course she'd figured it out when I walked in with Winston. "The chief has requested discretion pending advising Paula's granddaughter," I said.

Alicia pinky-wiped a tear. "I understand. You're a dear, taking charge of Winston. Paula would approve."

I about choked on my denial. Paula would just as soon strike me with lightning.

Smaller than the Corgi by a lot, Misha still didn't hesitate as she approached Winston and rubbed her head against his side. Winston exhaled, his sadness evident, but at losing Paula or being stuck with me, I wasn't sure.

"Oh, you poor baby." Alicia rubbed his back and slipped him a treat. The dog swallowed it whole.

Alicia stood up, all business. "You know Winston is a royal Corgi."

"Like Queen Elizabeth's?" I asked. Everyone knew the late monarch had been a Corgi lover. She'd been pictured with the breed throughout her long reign.

"Yes. Paula often compared her dogs to the many royal photographs. Winston is a descendant from the same line as the late queen's Corgi, Susan, back in the 1950s." Alicia curtsied. "I suppose that makes him 'His Royal Highness.'"

I glanced at the short-legged mini-dog. Maybe that explained the dog's presence. I'm not sure what else I could call the pride I'd noted in every turn of his head and his solid stance. His continuous smile even dared me to accuse him of anything.

Sandy must've read my mind. "Winston is an American dog."

I had no idea how to respond to that.

Alicia continued. "He is one of a kind. The Pembroke Welsh Corgi's breed standard doesn't include blue eyes, which means even though Winston is a purebred, Paula could never show or breed him."

"How does that happen?" Since my aunt bred Cavalier King Charles Spaniels, I understood some quirks occurred, but an eye color issue? My gaze fixed on Winston's haunting eyes.

"Karma, I guess." Alicia's nod and namaste hand position didn't help. I couldn't believe a dog had a destiny.

"You have a noise-cancelling headset, right?" Alicia asked.

I did, for air travel, but it would work even better than a

standard headset for blocking out Winston's barking. I couldn't hear a thing wearing it.

"Winston is partial to bunnies." Alicia fished a floppy-eared squeak toy out of the bag and pointed to the floor.

The Corgi plopped on the tile, his stomach on the ground and all four legs spread. What the...?

"It's called splooting. It's a signature Corgi move," Sandy explained.

"He does that for fun?" Wow! I'd never seen that before.

Alicia's laugh came out as a snort. "He does. I think he likes the feel of the cool tile on his belly. The toy focuses his attention."

Sandy squeezed between me and Winston. "Use the bunny toy for behavior modification."

I got it. Correct bad behavior. I eyed Winston. His head toss seemed far too innocent.

Alicia offered Winston the toy. The Corgi *arf*'d and took the long-eared, fluffy white toy in his mouth.

The first high-pitched squeak got my attention. The rapid-fire second, third, and fourth started my eye twitch. Did this dog do anything quietly?

At least he wasn't barking. "I understand he likes puzzles too."

Alicia's ear-to-ear grin scared me. This was going to cost me big-time, I realized, as she motioned me to follow her past the racks of froufrou doggie duds to what could only be described as a toy store.

I'm not sure if my eyes were bigger than Winston's baby blues when his shopping spree commenced. Every glossy box he nosed ended up in a basket for purchase. Okay, I admit it. Once I got over the sensory overload, it was kind of fun discovering the colorful flip-and-slide beach-inspired games, teaser balls to hold treats, and hide-and-seek squeaker puzzles. The peanut butter–flavored bubbles had to be my personal favorite. Who knew?

"This should keep Winston busy," Alicia said as she rang up my purchases. "He's pretty vocal. He talks too, you know."

He does? I spoke without thinking. "Can he tell me who killed Paula?"

"Paula was murdered?" Alicia's hand covered her mouth.

Now I'd done it. "You can't tell anyone."

"I won't. Paula told me digging up stuff on the relay station was dangerous. Do you think she was killed for that?" Instant anger concentrated in her clenched fists. "Why does your aunt want to pursue it?"

Because it was the right thing to do, I thought, but didn't voice that opinion. I needed far more information. Time to take notes. Barkviewians were clearly taking sides. I found pink Post-its when I patted my pockets. Sandy automatically handed me a pen. "Did Paula say why it was dangerous?" I asked.

"No. I did see her shaking her walking stick at Jordan yesterday, though. It was impressive."

No doubt a five-foot centenarian cowing a lanky six-foot-plus-a-bunch, shaggy-haired, beach-blond surfer had enhanced Paula's feisty reputation, but threatening the dive shop owner who'd stumbled across the sealed off World War II era room made no sense. I doubted Jordan Thompson had had a minute of peace since a leak behind the scuba tank filling tub had led to that discovery.

Paula's walking stick shake did demonstrate her annoyance, though. Was his inclusion a clue? I wasn't sure. "Did you hear what they were talking about?" Alicia's back door faced the Sea Dog Dive Shop's parking lot.

"No. The surf was too loud," Alicia replied. "Paula came in to pick up her regular squeak toy order yesterday afternoon

20

and told me things happened during the war no one needed to know about."

She had my undivided attention. "What kind of things?" Sandy started typing on her phone while I scribbled a note on a Post-it and stuffed it into my pocket.

"Paula refused to say. She was really worked up, though. She said this would change Barkview forever."

Talk about ominous. I made another note and stuffed it next to the other. The contents of the envelope waiting in my car really begged for my attention now.

Sandy took charge of my purchases while Winston and I headed for the exit. I opened the door and tripped right over the dog. Not a catch-yourself-in-the-doorway kind of fall either. Like a Torrey pine, I fell forward. Fortunately, I saved my nose from cobblestone burn at the cost of my palms instead. That would hurt in the morning.

Winston walked around me and licked my face. I spat fur out of my mouth and pushed him away. The tongue kept coming until Sandy pulled him back.

"Are you okay?" She held Winston by the collar.

I groaned and rolled over to sit on the dusty step. Between the dirt and the dog hair, my dry cleaner would have a heart attack. "He stopped in the doorway."

Sandy bit back a smile. "Dogs do that. You need to watch where you're going."

"Me!" I flashed Winston the evil eye. "He's a..."

Before I finished that thought, the Corgi broke free and somehow ended up in my lap, licking and wiggling. How could I be mad? He hadn't tripped me on purpose.

Sandy grinned. "You'll get used to each other. I'll put the toys in your car. You should take Winston on a walk before you drive back to the studio." I followed her gaze across the parking area to Jordon's dive shop.

She'd read my mind. A visit with Jordan could only help.

"I'll walk back to KDOG and start looking up World War II Barkview. Whatever Paula wants to keep secret has to be epic," Sandy said.

No argument from me. Maybe answers did lie in knowing more about Barkview during the war. Trust Sandy to dig in that haystack.

On the positive side, the dog wasn't barking. Head held high, Winston heeled perfectly, matching my pace and swinging his fluffy butt with all kinds of attitude—royal attitude, I reminded myself. I'd bet the Corgi could carry off wearing a crown.

We'd made it to the gas street lamp when my phone beeped. My fiancé's name popped up on the screen. Although Russ Hawl was an FBI consultant and security company owner, I had to wonder how he'd already heard about Paula.

"I didn't get a chance to call you." There really hadn't been time to share this morning's events with him. I was still reeling from them myself.

"The chief did. He's asked for my help investigating Paula's murder."

My stomach tightened. This just got far more complicated. "The ME confirmed it was murder?"

"Suspicious. I'm supposed to be the unbiased investigator."

"Unbiased? Has my aunt been ruled out as a suspect?" My fiancé could hardly be considered unbiased. What was Uncle G thinking?

"No. Witnesses say she and Paula had a heated argument earlier this week at City Hall."

This just got better and better. "My aunt argued with her earlier in the week about the historic building renovation?"

"Apparently. Paula considered the renovation digging up

the past. The evidence is all circumstantial. At this point we have nothing prosecutable," he said.

"Except in the court of public opinion." Which really was all that mattered in Barkview. That my aunt had known about Paula's objections shocked me. Aunt Char preached inclusion versus controversy. Why would she decide to pursue the project without Paula's agreement? Unless principle came into play... I swallowed a sudden lump in my throat. I really hated it when Aunt Char took the high road.

"I'm finishing up some paperwork now. I'll bring dinner by tonight. We can compare notes. I'll text you when I'm thirty minutes out." He hung up as I approached Surf Dog Scuba.

CHAPTER 4

Located on the east side of First Street among a grouping of 1920s Craftsman beach bungalows bordered by vibrant butterfly gardens, the green-trimmed dive shop faced the sparkling Pacific Ocean. The building had served as an early-warning radar station during World War II and a surfers' hostel in the 1960s and 1970s. Five years ago, Jordan Thompson and his chocolate lab, Baxter, had come to town for a photography convention. Although Jordan insisted the decision to stay had been mutual, most Barkviewians believed the lab's surfing skills ended any Rocky Mountain return. Over the years, Jordan enhanced his photography reputation to include award-winning oceanographic videography.

Winston bounded up the path, dragging me along behind. Those little legs could sure move. I had to sprint to keep up. Jordan met us at the screen door, where the Corgi sudden-stopped and barked rapid fire. I turned the tunes back on to take the edge off, glad Sandy had given me the headset earlier.

The barking didn't seem to bother Jordan any. He handed

me a Woofing Best Coffee cup and knelt to scratch Winston's belly with both hands.

I laced my fingers around the warm paper cup. The whiff of caramel cappuccino felt like a familiar hug. My first long swallow tempered my pounding heart as I leaned against the doorframe and watched Winston wiggle in ecstasy. Jordan clearly knew this dog. How well was the question. I removed the headset and raised the coffee cup. "Thank you for this. How did you know I was coming?"

"Winston always stops by after he goes to the Bow Wow Boutique."

According to Alicia, that had been weekly. "How well did you know Paula?"

"Paula recognized Baxter's surfing skills." Jordan stroked his scruffy beard. "She was a talented dog trainer. I regret that I started this and upset her."

"It's not your fault." I meant it. Who knew an eighty-year-old secret lay inside? "Can I see the room?"

Jordan gestured that I follow him. Winston preceded me through the door Jordan held open, pausing dead center. He took a long airborne sniff. I saw his nose just in time and caught the doorframe for balance. The doorway obstacle had done it again!

Before I could correct him, Winston's head toss indicated an all clear, and he stepped aside. As if I didn't know how to follow. Was this some kind of canine power play? Sandy had said Winston was a herding dog like Gem, the German Shepherd I'd previously dog-sat. That dog had policed my every move. At least the German Shepherd had been a sizable barrier. The Corgi barely registered in my peripheral vision.

I followed Jordan past the wetsuit racks to the back wall lined with vibrant underwater photography, featuring spirited harbor seals, gray whales breaching, and colorful garibaldis swaying amid giant California kelp. Behind the scuba tank filling tub, he swung open a plywood door hung in a cinderblock wall.

Jordan handed me a flashlight. "I guess this building had been a surfboard shop until the 1980s, when scuba became popular. The previous owner remodeled in 2008. I can't believe the room wasn't found then."

Me neither. Unless someone didn't want it to be found. Hmm. That bore investigation. I scribbled a Post-it note reminder and slipped it into my pocket. I followed Jordan inside. At least, I tried to. Winston nudged my calf aside. Not once, but twice. Enough. I high-stepped over the dog. The Corgi huffed and scooted in right behind me.

The dank smell got me right away. It had been closed up for a long time. What did I expect? No bigger than a modern walk-in closet with weathered cinderblock walls. I wondered how anyone had worked in the windowless hole. Talk about depressing.

"Was there any furniture inside?" I asked. I couldn't remember the details of the find.

"Yeah, it was kind of eerie," Jordan replied. "It looked like the room had been evacuated in a hurry. We found stained coffee cups on both of the metal desks and what looked like the remnants of a sweater hanging on a chair back. The file cabinet was bolted to the floor. The Historical Society had to use cutters to remove it. They took the rest of the furniture to research and refurbish too. The decoding papers were in good condition."

What could possibly have caused a hurried evacuation?

"For the record, I agree with your aunt," Jordan added. "Good or bad, Barkview's history needs to be told."

Of all people, Jordan knew that. His family had been unjustly run out of Barkview back in the 1920s. It had taken a hundred years to restore their good name. He was the first Tomlinson to return.

"Do you know why Paula objected?" I asked.

"I suspect she knew why we found World War II coded messages in the building."

I did a double take. That information had not been discussed at the City Council meeting. "What is that, exactly?"

"I asked Jennifer the same question," Jordan replied.

Barkview's librarian and president of the Historical Society, Jennifer Moore verified Barkview's history with National Archives precision.

Jordan continued, "During World War II the Japanese used various codes to send secret messages. The way she explained it, Purple was what they called their complex diplomatic code and JN-25 their naval codes, and a Katakana Morse code was used for basic radio transmissions."

That made no sense. "Japanese is based on symbols and characters. How do you even translate it into Morse code?" I asked.

"According to Jennifer, numbers were assigned to certain characters. The number sequences changed every three to four weeks."

My head pounded just thinking about it. "Wouldn't a local radio transmission station have coded messages to forward?"

"Jennifer said that the coded messages were sent to code-breaking stations. There was one at the Presidio in San Francisco for the West Coast. Not here in Barkview."

Could they have been mistakenly dispatched to Barkview or... "Did these messages originate in Barkview?" I asked, but I knew. My intuition kicked into high gear.

"I'm guessing Paula must've, at the very least, suspected there was a Japanese spy in Barkview," Jordan replied.

Talk about a bomb. A traitor in Barkview? In this no secrets town, how was that even possible? That Paula had known didn't surprise me. Her desire to cover it up did. I understood my aunt's decision to dig out the truth. I wouldn't let this secret remain hidden either.

The envelope from Paula just begged me to open it now. I thanked Jordan and walked Winston to my vehicle. The dog must've sensed my mission because he heeled perfectly and leaped into the passenger seat without incident.

I climbed in the driver's side and ripped open the manila envelope. Inside, I found a worn, brown leather book tied with a white ribbon. I opened the diary and read the first page Paula had penned a few months ago.

Dear Cat:

I leave this to you because I admire your tenacity. I am confident that no matter the consequence, you will ferret out the truth.

If that wasn't a call to action, I didn't know what was.

CHAPTER 5

My reporter's curiosity drove me as I motioned Sandy to follow me into my office the moment I arrived at KDOG. I managed to avoid tripping over Winston's room-block with a quick rabbit hop over him. He snorted his annoyance but followed me to my desk, where he splooted at my feet and closed his eyes.

Sandy sat in her usual chair with her tablet ready and her Jack Russell Terrier curled up at her feet.

"Let's hope Paula had some insights," she said simply.

I agreed. I read the first entry.

This story begins in 1940. My father trained dogs for Aaron Smythe, who sold them to the military. The Smythes' rise to prominence is a lie. Aaron Sr. buried a congressman's indiscretion in return for government construction and war contracts.

I walked the beaches every night thereafter to know what was real. My honor demanded it.

December 7, 1941, will, like President Roosevelt said, live in infamy. I remember the fear of Japanese invasion as if it was yesterday. I am ashamed I did not question the subsequent internment of Japanese Americans. We were at war. They were the enemy. That panic caused Barkviewians to turn on the Tanakas. The family farmed strawberries and flowers on the lagoon's north shore. They kept to themselves. Miyo, the Tanakas' oldest daughter, delivered the flowers to Barkview every morning. She studied math at State College. She was very exotic and untouchable. I don't know how Charles Smythe met Miyo, but I suppose every conflict must have a Romeo and Juliet. Back then, intermarriage was not done between a Japanese woman and an upper-class Smythe.

This is important because I did my bit as a radio interceptor during the war.

I was a civilian contractor, and Charles Smythe was the anchor clanker on the second dog watch. They called us Cookie and the Ace. I gathered and relayed radio transmissions from Hawaii to New York and intercepted and recorded (I mean, old-school wrote down on paper) local transmissions. I swore an oath of secrecy. I break that oath today.

Here are the facts as I know them. Coded

Japanese communications originating from Barkview began in November 1941. They paused when the FBI picked up Mr. Tanaka on December 7th, hours after the Pearl Harbor attack. And began again after his wife and daughters vanished two weeks later. Executive Order 9066 relocated the remainder of the Japanese population to internment camps on February 19, 1942. The coded Katakana radio communications continued until October 1942.

Sandy's fingers flew over her tablet. "The relay station was run by the Coast Guard. There is no record of Japanese communications originating in Barkview anywhere," Sandy insisted.

Could there really have been a traitor in town?

"According to this, civilian contractors manned many of the relay stations. In fact, many were women. Don't ask how, but the government had already discovered that women excelled at radio work."

I continued reading:

I figured once the Japanese were sent to the internment camps, we'd be home free, but the messages continued until October 1942, right after the Fish Creek Mountains Earthquake. Presumably the transmitter was killed, but the earthquake did little coastal damage. Just a few rocks fell off the cliffs. Two days later after a loud crash, Bark Rock sank eight feet into the Pacific Ocean. The bigger question remained. Who was the local contact?

31

Who would side with the enemy? My mission to find this traitor is now yours. I worked day shift at BIA Coast Guard Station and patrolled with my faithful Corgi, Ellie, at night. Oddly, the transmissions only occurred during my day shift, as if the traitor spoke only to me. Scuttlebutt had it that the brass figured me for a dope and file thirteened my reports.

On February 22, 1942, I intercepted a transmission on the 500 hZ wave in Katakana Morse.

Yes, I recognized it. I am not a fool like so many want to think. Something told me it was about a dog. When Charles arrived, I showed it to him. He paled when he read it. He questioned me about the transmission and agreed to pass it on. It was dark when I finally shoved off, so he escorted me to my car. Suddenly, Ellie barked and took off toward the beach. Despite the cloud-shrouded quarter moon and the full coastal black-out, both Charles and I saw the dog. In the gloom it looked like a long-legged Corgi. Charles recognized it. He whistled and called the dog by name. The dog responded and ran toward us. Up close, I recognized it too. It was Miyo Tanaka's Shiba Inu, who never left her side. Charles couldn't hide his concern. Was Miyo still in town? Or was someone else caring for the dog now?

Suddenly, the dog's ears perked. My Ellie yelped and buried her head beneath her paws. The Shiba Inu ran into the surf. Charles called it back. The dog just swam into the darkness, a silver cylinder attached to its collar visible in the moonlight. We saw no boat out there. Where was the dog headed? We figured a mousetrap was out there, lying in wait.

"A Japanese submarine right off the Barkview coast?" Sandy asked.

Had an invasion really been that close? I thought about the many anti-aircraft batteries once on the Barkview hillside. Where could a Japanese sub have possibly hidden from the vigilante outposts?

"How far can a dog swim?" How close can a submarine get to shore?

"Depends on the breed." Sandy referred to her phone. "Best case looks like ten minutes for a Labrador. A Shiba Inu would be about the same, and it's small enough to travel on a submarine too."

Where could the submarine have been? The military had sealed the offshore caves. The whole beachfront faced open water. "Could Bark Rock offer cover for a submarine?"

"A courier dog could certainly swim to shore from there." Sandy typed like mad on her tablet. "According to Google, a number of Japanese submarines entered US waters on the West Coast in early 1942, including the I-10 sub near San Diego. The submarine was three-hundred-fifty-five feet long and had a hundred-man crew."

"No way Bark Rock could conceal that from the coastal

batteries."

"The I-10 was also equipped with a mini-sub and a Yoko-suka floatplane. In fact, the aircraft hangar was part of the conning tower."

Was it possible? Just how close had a Japanese invasion been? "I thought the Pearl Harbor attack was the only Japanese attack on US soil," I said.

Sandy's fingers flew across her tablet. Her whistle said it all. "Geez! On September 9, 1941, a Japanese floatplane dropped incendiary bombs on an Oregon state forest. And on February 23, 1942, a Japanese submarine targeted the coast of Santa Barbara and fired sixteen rounds on the Ellwood Oil Field. There were also attacks in the Aleutian Islands, and about 300 balloon bombs were found along the coast."

All good reasons to fear invasion.

"Pretty brilliant plan. Who'd question a dog courier in the dog-friendliest city in America?" Sandy asked.

I agreed. "That had to be insider information. Paula was right. Someone living in Barkview in the 1940s was a traitor."

"Did Paula know who?" Sandy asked.

I finished the letter.

The patrol busted us. I'd broken curfew, and Charles had abandoned his duty station. We had an explanation, but Charles reached for my hand. I let him. We played moonstruck lovers so well we were married two weeks later. Charles shipped out in March. He transferred to saltwater cowboy duty. We weren't dead nuts on each other. We'd protected those we loved. Charles protected Miyo, and me, well, the only person who could've trained that dog was my father. Why this all matters is tied to a man named Henry Jones who disappeared from the Old Barkview Inn. The trail begins there.

Charles was killed when the USS Indianapolis sank. Oddly, I never really felt his loss. The Navy returned his dog tags, but not the St. Christopher pendant his mother had given him. In his personal papers I found this symbol and a note that said, "Forgive me. I did it for love."

I blinked to be sure I wasn't hallucinating. Drawn on the paper was the same phoenix symbol I'd been hunting for two years—the same symbol that marked the location of the long-lost Douglas Diamond.

CHAPTER 6

Sandy's whistle said it all. "Never saw that one coming."

Me neither. On the plus side, the long-lost diamond's hiding place existed in 1942, and we had a new place to search. "Bark Rock doesn't have a beach on the back side," I said.

Sandy exhaled her frustration. "Not so fast. No beach exists today, but that doesn't mean it wasn't there in 1925. Didn't Paula say something about Bark Rock sinking eight feet after an earthquake?"

I flipped back a few pages for confirmation. "Yeah. In October 1942." Still seemed like a long shot.

"That's some quest Paula left you. Where do you even start to look for a traitor from eighty years ago?" Sandy asked.

Inspiration would be a good thing about now. Short of that, sharing ideas had to be the next step. Too bad no conversation starter came to mind. "I'll read through the rest"—I held up the book—"tonight and see what other clues Paula left."

"Could Paula have been murdered by someone protecting

the traitor's identity?" Sandy asked. "The traitor is long dead. How could exposing them change anything today?"

"If Aaron Smythe's involvement comes out, it could bring a media circus down on Adam Smythe's congressional campaign." Chelsea, Adam's daughter and campaign manager, was going to have kittens over this. With all the former mayor's questionable practices in office, could something from his family's past derail his election? The question was, how far would Adam Smythe go to keep his campaign on track?

"Or not. Seriously, good or bad news in politics is still free press. No one is going to care if his great-great-uncle gave the Japanese information eighty years ago because of what amounted to a lost love. In fact, it might even help his campaign to address something important like racism."

Granted, Adam had run an uncharacteristically vanilla campaign, sidestepping controversy, which had to be Chelsea's doing. In the past, he'd embraced sensationalism.

I checked the time. "I'd better talk to Aunt Char. Can you reach out to Jennifer? Let's see if she has additional information on the Katakana code-breaking teams."

Sandy nodded. "I'll also see what I can find on Charles Smythe and the Tanaka family."

Winston must've agreed with my plan since he nudged my leg. "You should walk to City Hall," Sandy suggested. "He can get a little rambunctious if he gets bored."

One look at the Corgi's dancing blue eyes, and I felt fear. Not the run-for-your-life kind, but the what-mischief-are-you-planning kind. Sandy really was dog-clairvoyant. How else could she have read Winston's needs so accurately? I quickly leashed him. No sense taking any chances. I liked my traditional office exactly the way it was.

I even paused in the doorway to allow Winston to pre-sniff our exit. No need; the Corgi jerked me right out the door and

37

mush-dogged me to the sidewalk fire hydrant, where he pulled me to the left and then the right, finally stopping dead right in front of me. With nowhere else to go, my foot connected with his body, and I stumbled onto the nearby bench. I wasn't hurt, but I felt every eye in town on me. I could see the headline now: "Corgi Walking Cat."

Ugh! Time to master dog walking. I tightened Winston's leash and commanded him to heel. Winston tossed his head and smiled at me. I expected a fight. Instead, he obeyed, and we walked two blocks east on Oak to City Hall—if you could call that walk-trot-sniff anything but a mosey. I wanted to blame his short legs—he did take four steps to my one—but for a dog that was supposed to have tons of energy, he took his sweet time.

Constructed from local sandstone brick with a pitched roof and elegant redwood accents, City Hall epitomized the unique elegance of Barkview. Inside, I climbed the high-glossed oak staircase and followed the antique wall sconces to the mayor's office fronting Oak Street.

Dressed in a classic navy Dior suit and seated behind her ornate executive desk, Aunt Char looked more like a reigning Nordic monarch than a beach city mayor. Renny, her champion Cavalier King Charles Spaniel, sat sphinx-style on a chair beside her. Behind her a picture window framed by cut-glass side panels overlooked the period gas lampposts holding flower baskets exploding in early autumn colors.

Winston didn't wait for an introduction. He ripped the leash from my hand and leaped toward Aunt Char, barking nonstop. I reached for my headset's volume toggle. A single, decisive Cavalier bark ended the chaos and froze everything. Winston's outburst concluded with a whimper. He dropped to his stomach, all four legs grounded, his perpetual smile somehow muted.

Renny's head toss reprimanded me. Maybe I should've corrected the Corgi's behavior versus turning up the volume switch. I preached dog-owner responsibility daily. Funny how perceptions changed when you're in the middle of it. Until Paula's granddaughter claimed him, responsibility for Winston's behavior fell to me. I popped the headset out of my ears. Time to take responsibility.

Aunt Char crouched beside Winston to scratch his ears, in a pencil skirt, no less. I'd fall right on my face. "It really is all about being the alpha," Aunt Char advised me.

Alpha, huh? I glanced from my aunt to Renny, who licked her paw with deliberation. Far be it from me to question who ruled that relationship.

"Can Renny stay with me for a few days?" I could live with the dog's queenly airs if she controlled Winston's barking. In all fairness, Renny had earned her attitude. A three-time Barkview best-in-show winner, the fourteen-pound Blenheim Cavalier's pedigree outclassed my mixed-up European heritage any day.

Aunt Char's laughter drew mine. "You are welcome to ask her."

Renny's head toss said I was on my own. Thanks a lot.

"Winston really is a sweetheart," Aunt Char insisted.

When he was quietly lying on his back, feet quivering as she scratched his belly, I could agree.

"How are you two getting along?" Aunt Char asked.

"That dog is a serious tripping hazard. He stops in every doorway." My abused shins and palm seconded that statement.

Aunt Char didn't bother to hide her smile. "You do tend to charge into things, my dear. Think of Winston as a pause-and-consider kind of guy."

I'm sure that said something not-so-flattering about me. "Biggest issue is Russ. He's going to sneeze his head off."

Aunt Char didn't pause her scratching. "I thought the allergy shots were working?"

I picked a glob of fur off my pants for show and tell. "This pushes the limits."

"Brushing the dog well before Russ arrives should help." In a fluid motion I could never quite master, Aunt Char stood. "Tea?"

I nodded. Although I was a true coffeeholic, the smell of my aunt's coconut oolong tea brewing did bring back comforting memories. It was a part of her afternoon ritual. Aunt Char poured the tea and added a dollop of cream into each of the delicate china cups. "I understand Paula entrusted you with her quest."

I nodded and plopped into the plush desk chair. "Uncle G told you?"

"Heavens, no. Paula's murder is an ongoing investigation. He must remain objective." Trust Aunt Char to watch out for everyone but herself. "I asked Paula to give you her notes. The burden of keeping this secret was haunting her. She needed closure."

"That's why you voted to continue the historical verification." Of course Aunt Char, the psychiatrist, had done the right thing for someone in need—the only thing that would help Paula.

"Yes. I went to see her last night to assure her you would be discreet."

"Me, discreet?" I croaked. I believed in the truth. Maybe not at all costs, but..."We're talking about possible treason."

"Treason?" Aunt Char almost choked on her tea. She hadn't known the details. "World War II was a contentious time, my dear. Americans were imprisoned for no other reason than their ancestors came from Japan."

"We were at war. If Paula was right, someone in Barkview was sending messages to the enemy. Are you sure you want to know who it was?" Given that she professed to enjoy ignorance, I wondered exactly what she hoped to gain.

"That was a lifetime ago," Aunt Char explained.

"This is Barkview." Need I say more?

"You know that I believe we should all be judged on our own merits, not on those who have come before."

"Ideally, yes. I agree, but this is Barkview," I repeated. Family history mattered here. Too much, in my opinion.

"Paula did not have it easy. She was a war bride and widow left with a young son to raise," Aunt Char continued.

"She married a Smythe. Financially, she was well taken care of. To her credit, she raised a talented and honorable son. Many other women were not so fortunate."

Aunt Char sipped her tea. I tensed for the zinger. "There have been many rumors regarding the Smythes over the years. Whatever Paula was hiding, I am sure, relates to her first husband, Charles Smythe."

My tea sloshed over the rim. "A Smythe, the traitor?" Paula did think Charles had feelings for Miyo...

"I don't know. I do know Charles will never have an opportunity to defend himself." I braced myself as Aunt Char sat back in her chair. "You have a lot on your plate, and we will get to that, but right now I want you to be his advocate. To prove he either did or didn't do it."

Solve an eighty-year-old mystery? Not much of an ask here. Oddly, I should've felt an I-can't-possibly-get-it-all-done kind of panic, not crazy anticipation. Somehow I'd manage.

"Paula's murder tells me someone else doesn't want the

truth told," I said. Someone with something substantial to lose.

Aunt Char nodded. "I asked the chief to include Russ in this case. He will protect you."

No doubt, and ask me yet again why I delayed setting our wedding date. I should've guessed Aunt Char played a part in the decision. "I'm not going to choose a wedding date any faster..."

The psychiatrist in Aunt Char couldn't help herself. "Good heavens, I'm not rushing you. You and Russ need to make that decision. By the way, I drove by your new home. The pickleball net was hung this morning."

No pressure in that comment. Right? I loved to play pickleball. A court in my own backyard had been a major plus for me. I glanced at the spectacular Barklay engagement ring Russ had put on my finger a few months ago. In addition to the diamond, Aunt Char had insisted we move into the home she had lived in as a newlywed. Three switchbacks farther up the hill from Paula's, our new home was undergoing some much needed updating in preparation for when I finally chose a wedding date. Don't ask me what I was waiting for. Russ and I belonged together. My mind knew it. I was even dealing with the secretive nature of his business better. *Better* being the key. The man did the job government agencies either couldn't or wouldn't do. At least, that's what my reporter's mind imagined every time he used the "It's need-to-know" answer regarding his daily activities. Any wonder my uncertain inner voice needed reminding that I trusted him from time to time?

I chose to not take the bait and stayed on topic. My insecurities weren't the immediate problem. "I will need to share Paula's information with Uncle G and Russ."

Aunt Char nodded. "Of course. I can weather being the primary suspect for a while. Do be quick about it, though. I hope to announce Barkview's code-breaking past before Election Day."

That she intended to help Adam Smythe's congressional election didn't really surprise me. I almost warned her to be careful what she asked for. I'd dig up the information if I could. The events had occurred eighty years ago. Who knew if any evidence still existed? The real question was, what would she do if what I discovered proved damaging to Barkview?

CHAPTER 7

I took Sandy's advice about focusing the Corgi's excess energy and walked the four blocks from City Hall to the Old Barkview Inn. Just to clarify, *I* walked. Winston ambled two blocks and then plopped down on the cobblestone sidewalk with his front paws anchored. No amount of praise or treat bribery motivated him to move again. I felt like a parent dealing with a silent tantrum. Ordering him to walk did no good either. Winston just cocked his stubborn head and wiggled at me. I opted for expedience, scooped all forty-five pounds of him into my arms, and carried him the rest of the way to the iconic hotel. Ugh! My aching back took issue with winning through positive reinforcement and perseverance.

The stately Old Barkview Inn occupied several downtown blocks. Built in 1890, the elegant sky-blue building accented by white gingerbread trim was understandably the most photographed building in Barkview. In addition to serving as the setting for numerous Hollywood productions, the establishment had, over the years, hosted heads of state from around the globe. Inside the marble entryway, the hand-carved mahogany ceilings and stained-glass masterpieces demanded admiration.

When seeking information relating to the Inn, my best source had to be Will Oldeman, the oldest continuous employee and the most well-informed. I headed across the polished wood lobby to the Centurion Otis 61 elevator. Originally powered by steam, the ornate wrought iron museum piece had been converted to electric in the early 1970s.

Dressed in starched dark tails and a Victorian striped waistcoat, the ancient elevator operator stood with a pride that went deeper than longtime employment.

"Welcome, Miss Wright, Master Winston." He crouched to scratch the Corgi's ears. "What can I do for you?"

I smiled. "This is a bit before your time."

Will's Groucho brows arched.

"Do you know anything about a person going missing in February 1942?"

I expected surprise, even a you-can't-be-serious brow arch, not a resigned kind of exhale. There was way more going on here.

Will looked everywhere but at me before finally speaking. "I checked my grandfather's records. You know he managed the Inn during the war."

I nodded. Will's family had either owned or operated the hotel since its groundbreaking two centuries ago. "A fine family tradition."

"Yes." His hand lovingly stroked the elevator door. "Many hotels were taken over by the government and converted into housing and hospitals back then. My grandfather convinced the military he could manage the resources more effectively."

Undoubtedly, a born-and-raised hotelier could. "How did he do it?" While excess characterized the 1920s, the 1930s and 1940s had been downright tight.

Will's crossed arms had "lecture" written all over them. I settled in. "The hotel was a different place during the war. It housed pilots and families of officers. Visiting mothers, fathers, and wives booked the rest. He planted a victory garden and grew vegetables they served in the dining room. He even brought in milk cows."

I cracked a smile. Grazing livestock in the formal English garden? "Lucky folks who ended up here."

"Wartime changed the Inn. Blackout curtains allowed no light in or out. Sandbags sheltered the entrances. Rolled barbed wire fencing protected the shore from landing parties."

Not exactly a vacation paradise. Who would crave a seaside retreat with the Japanese threatening invasion, anyway? "At least the food..."

"Sugar, butter, and meat were rationed."

I swallowed hard. "Afternoon tea?" Only the best part of staying here.

"Afraid not. Henry Jones was in residence from February 20 to February 26, 1941. He borrowed a rowboat and did not return. A week later, a Coast Guard officer returned a repainted boat. Claimed that the Coast Guard recovered it three miles offshore. My grandfather was told Jones would not be returning."

"Why?"

Will shrugged. "My grandfather was a man of few words."

Unlike his grandson. "Was there ever an investigation?"

"There was nothing to investigate. The Old Barkview Inn's official registration pages from that time period are missing."

"Missing? How is that possible?" The Inn's guest registry resided in the Barkview archives.

"The same Coast Guard officer who returned the boat tore out the registration pages."

It sounded a lot like a cover-up. "Then how did you know Henry Jones was here?"

"Granddad kept private records."

Now that was interesting. A secret set of books listing who was and who wasn't in residence and when. Imagine the liaisons that book exposed. Will changed the subject before I could pounce on that thought.

"About a year after Paula's son Charles Jr. passed, she came to me asking if someone had disappeared from the Old Barkview Inn around the time Haruto Yamaguchi died."

My turn to be confused. "Michael Yamaguchi's relative?" Michael owned and operated Kanine Karate.

"Yes. His great-uncle was killed in a fishing accident at the beginning of March 1942."

I blinked. Paula had waited a long time to ask that question. "You discovered the missing pages in 1992?"

Will sniffed and focused on Winston, avoiding my gaze. I'd never realized that Will was an equal opportunity informant before. What was I missing? While Will freely answered questions, he rarely offered information, making asking the right question critical. "Why did she want to find out about this man?"

"The Coast Guard officer who returned the boat and took the guest pages was Charles Smythe," Will replied.

Her husband. Suspicious behavior, but had Charles been following orders or covering up something else? My best source for military history had to be Uncle G.

I thanked Will and headed back to KDOG. Fortunately, Winston herded me the two blocks there himself, nudging my calf every time I was about to collide with someone strolling along the boardwalk. Good thing too. A million possibilities filled my mind, none of them good.

Had Henry Jones seen the Japanese submarine and been

killed for it? But by whom? The Japanese? The Barkview traitor? Paula had already admitted that Charles Smythe had
committed treason to protect Miyo; would adding murder
matter? Could I prove anything at this point in time anyway?

No sense risking eavesdropping, so I waited until I could
close my office door before calling Uncle G.

"You want me to find out if the military found a John Doe
eighty years ago during wartime?"

Said out loud—even without his incredulous tone—it
sounded pretty insane. The military usually declassified files
after fifty years. If they existed, wouldn't Paula have found
them? Maybe there was no body to be found. "I'm not crazy.
Will has a copy of the original guest registry showing Henry
Jones checking in on February 20, 1942. The curious thing is
that the official registration records are missing. I don't mean
lost either. They were ripped out of the guest book."

Uncle G's hesitation spoke volumes. "How do you know
Henry Jones was his real name and he was really at the hotel?"

Good point. No one needed an ID to check in back then. "I
guess I don't. I'd like to know what happened to the personal
effects that were supposedly taken from the missing man's
room."

Uncle G turned all business. "Is that what Paula wanted
you to look into?"

"So it seems."

His cough barely hid his annoyance. "I can't promise
anything."

"I understand." I did. Talk about a statistical longshot.
"Russ told me that the coroner ruled the preliminary cause of
Paula's death as suspicious. Could she have hit her head from a
fall?" Winston's uncanny ability to be underfoot really made
me wonder if her injury had been an accident after all.

"Doubtful."

Scratch that hope. I thanked him for the information as Sandy and Jack popped into my office. That glint in Sandy's blue eyes screamed trouble. "According to the *Bark View*, Haruto's boat was lost on February 25, 1942. His body washed up on the beach on March 1st. There is no record of a Henry Jones doing anything in Barkview during that time."

"Why would Paula connect the two?" A Caucasian American could hardly be misidentified as a Japanese American.

"Haruto's remains were identified by a family ring on his left hand. Floating in the water for several days really affected the body's decomposition," Sandy explained.

Ugh! That thought messed with my mind. I got Paula's suspicions. Two people missing or presumed dead around the same time seemed pretty coincidental.

"The connection is still weak. Except for Paula's information and Will's secret duplicate registration book, there's no other evidence Henry Jones existed."

I agreed. "Can you find out anything about Henry Jones?"

"You're kidding, right? Almost six percent of the population is named Jones. We have nothing to limit the search."

True. Was the name just bad luck or by design? My intuition wasn't really saying yet.

"I think our best chance is to find the Tanaka family." Sandy tapped on her tablet. "The thing is, I don't see them listed at any internment facility."

"They just vanished?" I asked. Now that was odd.

"The right of habeas corpus was suspended in 1941. I know we were at war, but Big Brother with no limitations scares me." Sandy shuddered.

Agreed. "I'll visit Michael at Kanine Karate." If anyone knew what happened to the Tanakas, he would. "His father lobbied for Japanese reparations. There's even a picture of President Reagan signing the bill in his dad's dojo."

49

I'd seen it often enough during my karate phase. I checked the time. I could easily get home, re-iron pleats in my gi and get to the dojo before evening classes commenced.

An alert pinged on Sandy's phone. "The forecast has been updated. The Santa Ana winds are predicted to start tomorrow."

Anticipation hummed through me. Was the Douglas Diamond finally in reach? "I want to check out the backside of Bark Rock." Why not? We'd looked everywhere else for that phoenix-like symbol.

"Best to be stealthy," Sandy suggested. "If you take Winston out on your paddleboard, no one will suspect a thing."

No kidding. Treasure hunters' eyes seemed to be everywhere lately. "Bring Jack too. Two sets of eyes can't hurt."

Sandy nodded. "I'll meet you at eight."

I glanced at the fur-rug hugging my feet. The two of us sharing a paddleboard? I eyed him critically. Granted, he did have a low center of gravity, but since when did I share a board?

Winston lifted his head and Corgi-smiled at me. What had I just agreed to do?

CHAPTER 8

Kanine Karate hadn't changed much since I'd been a student there. Black mats still covered the floors, and serene landscapes dotted the walls. The glass and black-lacquered trophy case had expanded to include an Olympic bronze medal won in 2020 by one of Michael's advanced students in Tokyo.

Today, a lone yellow-belted student practiced in front of the mirrored wall on the mat. I recognized the twenty-move Kihon kata after the eighth step. The woman's fluidity impressed me. I'd struggled with the disciplined katas. The choreographed moves required serious memorization. Unlike the hula, which told a story, a kata's moves had no discernable reasoning, at least to me. The sparring kept me coming back. I admit, I liked taking down a larger opponent. Maybe too much.

Winston growled as we approached the doggie care staff to the right of the entrance. This had to be one of the few places in Barkview where your dog met you at the exit. Not that I objected. Canines underfoot in a dojo would be catastrophic.

The moment I tried to hand off Winston's leash, he jerked it right out of my hands and Corgi-ran—or whatever you'd call that weird flying-leap-sprint thing he did with all four feet off the ground at one time—toward the student mid-kata. OMG! The yellow belt around her waist fluttered like a matador's cape.

My warning stuck in my throat. The dog's springboard jump gave him just enough height to catch the flapping belt in his mouth. He swung like a kid suspended on a rope, his momentum taking the small-statured woman down.

Michael Yamaguchi beat me to her side. Like his father, Michael had earned the Hanshi title. A seventh-degree black belt, he was the guy you wanted next to you in a dark alley. Standing a little over six feet tall, with dark, almond-shaped eyes and a lithe, muscled body, he wore his black-belted white gi with a peaceful confidence I wished I'd mastered. Only his dark hair, now sprinkled with silver, hinted at his age.

The girl sat cross-legged on the mat, holding her hand out for Winston's sniff. The dog's growl did not waver.

Michael interrupted my self-introduction. "*Osu, Koneko.*" His slight brow arch acknowledged my gi.

Of course he'd noticed. Nothing got by his too-knowing gaze. I'd dressed in the customary white cotton kimono-style jacket and drawstring pants, glad for the extra girth. Not that I'd gained a ton of weight. That happy-relationship-weight-gain just snuck up on me. Today I'd defied tradition by folding the gi right over left and tying the purple belt left over right. During my three years of study, I'd done the same thing.

Michael had always called me "little Cat" because mischief found me at every turn. Seriously, I didn't go looking to rebel. It just sort of happened. "*Osu.*" I tapped my right fist into the open palm of my left hand, bowed slightly, and corrected my dress. I'd never actually intended disrespect. I simply hadn't been able to wrap my mind around the importance of tradition.

I turned to the girl. "I am..."

"Cat Wright." She brushed Corgi fur off her hand before offering it. "Hana..." Winston's sudden bark made Hana's words hard to hear. "I'm a political analyst on the Smythe campaign."

"Have we met?" I asked. Up close, she was older than I'd first thought. I'd have remembered this exotic beauty. Even with her black hair tightly braided, her porcelain complexion set off slightly Asian features complemented by stunning blue-gray eyes.

"Not personally. I've been following your aunt's career. I hope she knows what an asset you are to her." Likely more of a hindrance, but Hana's smile seemed genuine enough. The world of political public scrutiny still surprised me at times.

Michael saved me from responding. I mean, how do you respond to that? "She's a postgraduate student at Georgetown."

"*Arigato gozaimasu.*" Hana bowed respectfully, forward bend perfectly creased. "My master's thesis focuses on election strategies. Your aunt's rejection of negativity in campaigning was inspiring."

"Aunt Char inspires many people." What else could I say? Hana intrigued me. The woman attended a big East Coast school. Why work on a small-town congressional campaign across the country? "Do you know Winston?" I wasn't exactly certain what Winston's *grrr* meant.

"I imagine he smells Saki, my Shiba Inu." I recognized Hana's goofy dog-crazy grin right away. She fit right in here.

"I am sorry to hear about Paula Powell. She lived a remarkable life," Hana continued before I could ask. "I had hoped to speak with her regarding the political situation in Barkview. Somehow we must return to small-town values to improve our national situation."

53

No argument from me. Paula's biography had brought many people to her doorstep with questions.

Michael refocused the discussion. "Your practice looked good, Hana. Your focus on the third punch 'kiai' seemed to wander."

"Yes, *Hanshi*." Hana unfolded her legs and stood. The doggie day care folks took charge of Winston.

Focus? I thought it had looked very good. But good didn't cut it at Kanine Karate. Michael turned his know-too-much eyes on me. "You think you are ready for your next step?"

Was he talking about karate or my life? The pressure from not choosing a wedding date seemed to come from everywhere now. Or was I just being paranoid? The man's infuriating insight had always made me crazy. I'd come to the dojo within a month of my doctor's release from the Pit Bull attack, determined to learn self-defense. As if martial arts could be mastered in a few short months. Thanks to Michael, I'd learned far more than escape moves. "You have always been wise," I said honestly.

His nod acknowledged my compliment. "And you are destined to find your way."

What did that mean? He'd always said karate was a state of mind enhanced by your commitment. Best to avoid that thought. "I have come to speak to you about your great-uncle."

Michael's grimace surprised me. My curiosity peaked as he motioned for me to follow him across the practice mats to his private office, located opposite the entry in a quiet corner. I wondered what direction today's lesson would take.

Michael got right to the point. "Why are you interested in a man who passed eighty years ago during a time better forgotten?"

A fair question. I shifted in the plastic chair to face a small lacquered desk. In here, Japanese Shogun weaponry replaced calm landscapes on the walls. "I'm looking into the Tanaka family's situation in 1942. I understand your family grew strawberries east of the highway."

"Yes. My grandfather was *Issei*. He arrived in 1934. My grandmother was a picture bride in 1936."

I cringed. I couldn't help myself. Marrying a man she'd never met and moving to a foreign country took real guts.

Michael shook his head. "To a twenty-first-century American the custom would seem barbaric. It was common practice in Japan at the time. Respect for family and tradition remains strong today."

Fascinated, I had to ask, "Is 'saving face' still a thing?"

He inhaled. "Modern Japan is evolving."

Maybe too much for Michael? I wasn't sure. "Getting back to 1942."

"My family was moved to the Poston Internment Camp in March 1942. Miyo Tanaka was my great-uncle's *miai*, or promised bride."

Miyo had been engaged? "Did she keep a diary?"

Michael shrugged. "They never married. I don't know what happened to Miyo. Her family disappeared in December 1941."

"Without a word?"

"The story goes that some government men came for her father. The family disappeared a few weeks later. My great-uncle tried to find her, but it was a hard time for the Japanese. He was killed in a boating accident in February 1942," Michael explained.

Interesting. Paula's notes inferred a relationship between Charles Smythe and Miyo. I swallowed. Had Miyo been the traitor? "I understand your great-uncle was identified by a ring."

Michael nodded. "It was a jade family ring that belonged to

55

his father. It was said Haruto's fishing boat was hit by another boat. The boat must've sunk. What remained was..."

No need to explain more. I got it. The timing still bothered me. "It was a dark time in American history." I pointed to the photograph of Michael's father holding the pen used to sign the 1988 Civil Liberties Act paying restitution to the interned Japanese. "Your grandfather had to have been pleased."

Michael shook his head. "He was not. His generation wanted to forget the war. My father's demanded acknowledgment."

"Yet your father pursued it anyway." Not what I'd expect from a hierarchy based on elder respect.

"It was a generational disagreement. My father felt grandfather would understand eventually. He never did." That had to make family dinners uncomfortable.

"What about you?" I asked.

Pride showed in Michael's squared shoulders. "I am proud of my father's accomplishment. I hope by bringing the internment injustice to light, it does not happen again."

"I agree." I shifted in my chair. After his father's quest, would Michael admit if there had been a traitor in Barkview?

No hiding my dilemma from Michael's sharp gaze. "What did you come here to ask me, Cat?"

"I have information that there may have been a traitor in Barkview in 1942 still sending messages well into October. If all the Japanese were relocated by April 1942, who could have been sending them?"

"That was eighty years ago," Michael said.

"I know. There was also another man reported missing in February 1942. Someone named Henry Jones."

"An American? My family did not mix with visitors back then." Michael's frown indicated that the admission bothered him. It bothered me too. "What exactly do you want from me?"

56

"You know all the area families. Do any have old diaries or memoirs from the period?"

"Is this about the codebreakers?"

I nodded. Though it was more about something feeling wrong.

"Paula wanted the subject dropped. I agree with her. No good will come of digging up this past."

"I'd think you'd want this truth told. If only so it never happens again."

Michael exhaled. "I see no reason to tarnish Barkview's storied past. Yes, what was done was wrong, but the Japanese were compensated and laws have changed."

He seemed okay with it all. Why did my blood boil? "I don't expect to prove anything. I just want to know the truth."

"With Paula gone, no one lives who was there. You will only have biased words."

I nodded. "I would appreciate anything you can find."

"I will ask." Michael rose. "There is a confidence about you now. You are ready to complete your karate training."

His words shocked me. Three years ago he'd basically kicked me out of the program. Physically, I was light years behind now, but he knew it. It had never been about my muscular strength. I got it now. Four years of trying to prove him wrong had helped me find my inner peace. That and good wine. "I appreciate your offer, but I'm doing what I should be doing now."

Michael grinned. "You always were. You just needed to believe in yourself."

That he'd recognized that in me said a lot about his teaching skills. "If I am looking for a phantom traitor, where do you suggest I look?"

Michael scratched his chin. "Perhaps you should look closer to home."

I returned Michael's bow. Who could have possibly bene-fited from a Japanese invasion? Except for Aaron Smythe Sr., the man building military defenses and training facilities. I needed to chat with Chelsea Smythe.

I took charge of Winston and glanced at my phone as I walked to my Jag. Russ's text said he'd be over with takeout around 7 p.m. I ignored the Corgi hair cloud as I motioned the dog to jump into my front seat. If I hurried, I could get the green wine chilled before Russ arrived. The wine wasn't really Dr. Seuss green, of course. It's a wine from the Minho region in northern Portugal. Called "green" because it's only aged for a few months. The flavors complimented spicy Thai food perfectly. Although Russ hadn't specified, tonight was defi-nitely a spicy Thai food kind of night.

CHAPTER 9

Considering Russ's allergies, taking Aunt Char's advice and brushing Winston on the patio prior to his arrival seemed like a good plan. I mean, a Corgi was no puffy Bichon; even I could follow YouTube instructions to brush the dog in the direction of his fur. How many ways could there be?

Many, it turned out. The fiasco really was on Winston. The dog kept pulling away from me and sniffing oceanward. I got that he wanted to run in the sand, but there was no way I'd deal with hair and sand in my house. You'd think self-preservation would prevail and he'd just sit still since I wielded a weaponized pincushion loosely called a brush. When the torture device snagged his polar-bear-thick fur yet again, Winston had enough. He yelped and jerked backward, bumping my hand. I lost my grip, sending the brush sailing over the teak dining table. Like a precision torpedo, it direct hit a geranium container, shattering the ceramic pot. That the plant had been on its last leaf hardly mattered. The brush had delivered the deadly blow.

I ignored Winston's exasperation. Just wait until he saw

the lion's mane framing his neck. Any wonder I admired self-grooming cats?

I retrieved the brush, noting the dog-size hair ball stuck to the teeth. Well, mission accomplished at the cost of a plant, undoubtedly a more cost-effective option than a visit to the Fluff and Buff Salon.

I checked my watch. Ten minutes until Russ arrived. Not enough time to peek at Paula's diary, but enough to prep the wine. My taste buds tingled just thinking about the fruity effervescence. I motioned Winston inside. The dog tossed a catch-me-if-you-can look over his shoulder and darted for the gate. The leash stopped him a step short.

Ha! I'd foiled a dog. My celebratory *Yeah!* stuck in my throat. Winston's mischievous look promised retaliation. Our gazes locked, neither one of us breaking eye contact, until Winston's ears twitched and he took off inside, barking.

I dropped the leash and let him go, following more slowly behind to top off the animal-stemmed wine glasses. I smelled the peanut sauce the second Russ cleared the doorway. Yum. We really did read each other. Caught by the sexy sweep of his dark hair framing his blue-fire gaze, I melted into his kiss, responding to the feel of his well-defined swimmer's shoulders pressed against me. What was I waiting for? Marry the man already.

"Kiss me like that, and I'll never leave," he whispered against my neck. His rapid-fire sneeze killed the mood.

I shivered. Good thing Russ respected tradition—every last antiquated Barkview one.

He set the bags on the counter. I slid the wine glass into his hand and took a long sip of mine. The fresh, fizzy gooseberry essence filled my senses.

"What a day." Russ frowned as he scratched Winston's ears. Okay. The lion hairdo wasn't a long-term solution. I'd figure out how to tame it tomorrow. Russ wisely moved right into my kitchen to plate the meal on Serengeti-inspired dinnerware without a word.

No airborne Corgi fur had to be a win. I set the placemats and napkins on the counter bar. "Has the chief found Paula's granddaughter yet?"

"Not yet. What's the rush? You and Winston seem comfortable together."

I glanced at Winston splooted on the tile floor, one eye on Russ in the kitchen and the other on me. "Hmmm." What else could I say? The dog and I did have a sort of married-couple compatibility. "I worry about you."

"Me?" He eyed me oddly. "A little dog hair isn't going to kill me."

No, but the telltale redness in the whites of his eyes looked super uncomfortable. So much for brushing the dog helping to limit his allergies. "I really don't want you to suffer."

"The allergy shots are working. I'm fine."

Stoic to the end. "Really?" I'd hate to see no meds at work.

Russ chuckled. "Let's enjoy the pad thai. I ordered it with extra chili the way you like it."

Who could argue with noodles and shrimp stir-fried in a rich sweet-savory fusion sauce and dusted with crushed peanuts? Fork ready, I slipped onto the barstool and savored my first bite. "What would you do if I end up dog-sitting for a Saint Bernard?"

"You'd never accept that challenge."

Russ's confidence surprised me. "As if I have a choice." My dog experiences tended to find me.

"Saint Bernards slobber. Big globs of saliva everywhere when they shake their heads," Russ explained.

Double ick! Sheet-white had to describe my reaction. "Point taken." Silence stretched between us.

61

"The owners accepted my offer on the Fourth Street building. Blue Diamond Security's headquarters is officially relocating to Barkview."

"That was quick." I guess I should've been more enthusiastic. Russ had already executed his commitment to our life together. Why did I feel like the rug had been pulled out from beneath me? "Are you sure about the Victorian fitting your image?" While historic homes and Barkview went hand in hand, the look didn't exactly represent a high-tech security company.

"It's a differentiator."

"No kidding."

"I expected you to be happier. The remodel on the house"—Russ always called our new home in the Terraces "the house"—"is ahead of schedule. The contractor is estimating a mid-October move-in."

"Sandy will be happy to move in here early." I looked around my familiar townhouse and swallowed hard. I liked the status quo. Did that make me a closet neophobic?

"I'll keep my place down the street until..." He turned my stool to face him and wrapped me in a warm hug. "Hey. I'm not pushing you to choose a wedding date. We can slow the train down if that's what you want."

"It's not that." It really wasn't. Just thinking about planning one more thing made me want to hyperventilate.

Russ captured me between his thighs, his gaze locking with mine. "I know you're overwhelmed settling into the new job and looking for the Douglas Diamond."

I exhaled. I really hated it when he drilled right down to the root of the problem.

Russ smiled. "You know I'm fine if we run off to Vegas and have Elvis marry us, right? What I care about is you..."

"...doing the right thing." I finished the sentence for him.

"And having the big Barkview extravaganza like every Barklay heiress."

"The right thing is what you're comfortable with. Whether it's barefoot on a beach or in the Barkview church with all of your aunt's closest political allies, in the end we will be together." He cupped my chin in his hands.

The fire in his eyes said it all. I was an idiot doubting him. Nothing deterred Russ from a goal. "If it was just us, what would you want to do?" I asked.

He smiled. "It's not just us. I'm the prince consort at this event. You are the queen, my dear."

In a way, maybe, but his opinion did matter to me. "What I should do and what I want to do is not aligning." Why couldn't I just decide? I'd even flipped a coin about a hundred times.

"It will." Russ forked his dinner.

Did I ever wish I had his confidence? Fence-sitting poked you in uncomfortable places. Maybe I just needed a simple list of pros and cons.

I swear Winston's look dared me to try. What did I have to lose? A smile-up or smile-down list couldn't hurt.

"By the way, the murder weapon was Paula's walking stick," Russ announced.

Trust Russ to make his point and then refocus me with a single sentence. A smile-up point for him. Smile up, 1. Smile down, 0.

"You're sure it wasn't an accident? Winston is a stumbling hazard. I have the bruises to prove it."

"The angle of impact..." Russ's detailed velocity and arc demonstration went right over my head.

"So it had to have been a high-to-low overhead shot?" I asked, still not convinced. "How tall was the assailant?"

"Five feet ten to six feet tall. What's bothering you?" Russ asked.

Of course, Aunt Char in stilettos fit the profile. "It feels like a crime of passion." Hard-headed and opinionated, Paula had angered just about everybody at some point, but enough to murder her?

"It seems possible."

"My aunt is…"

"The primary suspect."

"You know she didn't do it." I watched his reaction over my glass.

"We follow the evidence." Spoken like the true investigator I admired. He'd ferret out the truth. He always did.

"The question is, what was Paula trying to hide?" I countered. Could Paula's quest for answers really have been a factor? What could possibly matter eighty years later? "Can you get Hiro Tanaka's FBI files from 1941?"

"You're serious?" His look questioned my sanity.

I wondered about it myself. "They should be declassified by now."

"If so, then the records are in the National Archives. What are you specifically looking for?"

"Apparently, the FBI arrested him on December 7, 1941, hours after Pearl Harbor."

"The FBI rounded up many influential community leaders at that time," he admitted.

"True. Habeas corpus had been suspended, but Hiro Tanaka couldn't have simply disappeared. Even more curious is that the Tanaka family vanished a few weeks later. There is no record of where they went."

"You think they were picked up by the FBI too?" Russ asked.

I nodded. "I have a feeling there's more to this. Hopefully, Paula's diary will lead me somewhere."

"I'll see what I can find," Russ said. "Chad Williams's

contact at the National Archives may be the better source, though."

I hadn't considered that. Would the *Finders Keepers Treasures* blogger and self-proclaimed Douglas Diamond expert help me? Although we'd shared a few Douglas Diamond–related adventures, he viewed me as a rival in the hunt for the diamond, mostly because he wanted the prize money. I just wanted closure.

"We should talk to your aunt tomorrow morning," Russ said.

"I'm committed to taking Winston paddleboarding in the morning."

Russ blinked. "You're going in the water in September? This must be related to the Douglas Diamond."

I couldn't get anything by him. "The Santa Ana winds are forecast to start tomorrow. Sandy figured Winston would provide an excuse for me to look around the backside of Bark Rock."

Winston's ears perked up at the sound of his name.

"Bark Rock? Do I want to know?" Russ asked.

"It's just a hunch." I explained the World War II dog-courier theory. "The only place close enough to conceal a Japanese sub would've been Bark Rock. Though all the hillside lookouts missing it doesn't make sense."

Russ poured the remainder of the wine into our glasses. "If I remember my history correctly, the Japanese had mini-subs on some of their I-class submarines."

Who remembered that stuff from high school?

Russ added, "It would've been close enough to San Diego naval station to intercept messages. Is there a cave on the backside?"

"Not that I know of. I suppose there could've been a small one there once upon a time. The Fish Creek Mountains earthquake in October 1942 coincides with the end of enemy chatter in Barkview."

"You're suggesting a rockslide eliminated the submariners' hiding place?"

"Maybe. The timing can't be a coincidence."

"I agree. You also tend to be accurate. Mind if I join you?" No missing the mischievous glint in his eyes. He was up to something. I felt it.

"You don't even like paddleboarding," I reminded him. Surfing, yes, but he'd called paddling boring.

"True. I do like a good laugh, though."

"At me or with me?"

"With you, of course."

The vision of Winston and me tumbling into the frigid Pacific Ocean just chilled me. I really wanted to be mad. "No GoPro." Social media posts could get out of hand.

He crossed his heart. "I'm only tagging along to keep you two afloat." I believed that. The man had a serious lack of faith in my abilities, not that I'd done anything to improve them either.

"I can always use someone to carry my board."

His sexy grin didn't alleviate my concern one bit. What had I just agreed to?

CHAPTER 10

I took Winston for a walk while Russ cleaned up. I had to love sharing household duties. Smile-up point for Russ. I accessed another smile-up point when I saw the note he'd left on Paula's diary before he left for his condo: "Enjoy." The man really did know me.Smile up, 3. Smile down, 0.

I microwaved a chamomile tea and changed into tiger-striped PJs. Naturally, Winston wanted up beside me after I'd settled into my favorite position on the couch. As I reached to assist him, he leaped over my shoulder, his nose prodding the diary. How those midget legs propelled him to twice his height still took me a minute to process. I noted the hair trail running the length of my pant leg. Nothing a washing wouldn't cure, I reminded myself, and scratched the thick coat around his neck with both hands. Was I on the verge of dog-hair tolerance? Never!

I pulled a few Corgi glitter strands off the book and shooed Winston away. A split in the leather's inner edge drew my eye as I opened the front cover. Had the seam been loose, or had

Winston disturbed it? This book belonged in Barkview's historic archives. Not destroyed in my hands.

I glared at Winston. Little good my look did: the dog blinked at me, innocent as a lamb.

I gave up to inspect the damage. Was that something silver hidden inside? I shook the book. A few loose pages rained around me, but I could hardly miss the Barkview Bank's safe-deposit box key that bounced on the sofa.

Winston's about-time huff stirred my curiosity as I placed the key on the wood coffee table. Whatever Paula had found she'd deemed important enough to secure. Curiosity gnawed at me. Too bad the earliest I could get inside the bank would be 9 a.m., but the time wouldn't matter if Paula hadn't added me as a signer. Otherwise, only her granddaughter could access it.

Great. Did I delay looking for the Douglas Diamond or accessing Paula's hidden information? Too much on my plate. A smile-down point. Maybe Russ's early-to-rise philosophy had merit after all. Not.

Smile up, 3. Smile down, 1.

Patience, I reminded myself and opened the book to the last entry I'd read. With any luck, there'd be more clues inside.

May 3, 1942: After the hoopla settled down I decided to put on my deerstalker and questioned my father about training Shiba Inus. He insisted he knew nothing, but his right eye twitched. The man can't bluff. His poker buddies must be blind.

I'll find the files. Charles and I own the Terrace's kennel and property now. Aaron Smythe deeded it to us as a wedding gift. My father moved into the house with me after Charles shipped out. A neat arrangement for us all.

May 5, 1942: I found the records on two Shiba Inus, both owned by Hiro Tanaka. My father's note "CP trained" could only mean "carrier pigeons." He'd done that once before for sisters who lived miles apart. I visualized the silver tube attached to the dog's collar. If the Shiba Inus carried notes, why continue sending coded radio messages? I thumbed through the remainder of Dad's cryptic notes. He noted no human trainers. That he'd charged double his US military fee confirmed the client wanted discretion.

The question was with Hiro Tanaka under arrest and all other Japanese descendants removed from town, who controlled the dogs now? Below I listed Barkviewians familiar with Dad's techniques. Someone is a traitor. The lie Charles and I told allowed them to continue. I must uncover the truth.

Aaron Smythe topped the list. But others could've been involved: Nell's great-grandfather or Will's grandfather had all lived in Barkview during the war. Paula's sleuthing skills were first class. How had she found the info during wartime and without the benefit of the internet?

June 1, 1942: I got my wrist slapped again for digging around, but confirmed that Hiro Tanaka *had served as an officer in the Imperial Japanese navy during the Great War on a Japanese aircraft carrier. He arrived in Hawaii in 1933.*

Aircraft carriers in 1918? I used my phone's browser to search. Sure enough, information popped up. Wow! Who knew?

I glanced at Winston snoring at my side, as my grandfather clock bonged eleven times. I dialed Sandy. It wasn't too late. By her own admission, she never slept anyway, primarily due to her Jack Russell Terrier.

Sandy answered on the second ring. "What's up, Boss?" I detected wariness in her tone. Not that I blamed her. Me calling late never ended well for her.

"Do you know anything about Japanese aircraft carriers during World War I? I saw something on the internet about a converted former British cargo vessel renamed Wakamiya."

I heard the telltale keyboard tapping in the background. "It appears to be a thing. The boat carried two Farman bombers launched from a small platform."

"That had to be small. World War I aircraft were basic." I knew far more than I ever wanted to about those planes after researching Skye Barklay's life story.

"The Hosho was the first official aircraft carrier, completed in 1922. The Japanese navy apparently used this ship to build its naval strategy leading up to World War II."

"Well, they nailed it. Aircraft carriers ruled in the Pacific theater."

"How does this fit with Paula's quest?" Sandy asked.

"I'm not sure." I explained the minimal information Paula had written about Hiro Tanaka. "Listen to this."

I don't understand why a ranking naval officer would leave Japan. Or why, after joining the Japanese fishing fleet, he would leave Hawaii to become a farmer in California.

"She was right. A ranking military man in 1933 Japan was at the top of the political food chain," Sandy said. "Let's see what happened to change his mind. *Hmm.* There was a failed military coup in 1932 after the Shanghai Incident."

"What was the Shanghai incident?" I asked.

"I'll send you a link. Basically, the Japanese military provoked anti-Japanese demonstrations that led to the May 15, 1932, assassination of the prime minister and the rise of military rule in Japan."

"Hiro could've been disenchanted with Japan," I suggested. People with strong moral codes often lost faith in politics.

"Talk about being a great asset for US intelligence."

No kidding. "If he was loyal to the United States. He could've also been a Japanese spy."

"If so, then why leave Hawaii? The US Pacific Fleet was at Pearl Harbor. San Diego was only a Reserve Depot and training area in the 1930s."

She had a point. "I agree. The family disappeared in 1941. Maybe they went back to Hawaii. The Japanese weren't interned in Hawaii."

"That makes no sense. Why were the mainland Japanese more dangerous than those in Hawaii?" I asked.

Sandy's *hmmm* warned of a pronouncement. "It's always about the economics. Thirty-three percent of the folks living in Hawaii were of Japanese ancestry."

Talk about a society coming to a screeching halt. "Maybe

Hiro returned to Japan. People just don't disappear in the USA."

"Maybe the trail is just lost," Sandy suggested.

"Wouldn't the fishing fleet in Hawaii be a perfect cover for a spy watching naval vessels? Can you find out what political groups Hiro Tanaka belonged to before he came to California?"

"That's a tall order. I'll try. I have a friend at UH."

Of course she did. Sandy had friends everywhere. "And it's only 9 p.m. there," I added.

"Your mother may be helpful as well," Sandy suggested.

"I thought of that." My stepdad's position as a Coast Guard commander in Hawaii did open some interesting doors. Was I ready to test my still-tentative relationship with my mother?

"But?" Sandy prodded.

"She's going to give me grief about the wedding date."

Sandy's chuckle escaped. "Someone has to."

That hurt. "You just want to move into my place."

"I do, but that's not the issue and you know it," Sandy said.

I did. Maybe I needed some tough love.

"Russ is moving his corporate headquarters to Barkview. What more do you want? Like it or not, life changes," Sandy said.

A million reasons why it shouldn't have to came to mind, none of them even worth repeating. "I know. I'll see you in the morning."

"Call your mother," Sandy said and hung up.

Winston's chin on my thigh somehow helped. I scratched his head, staring at the safe deposit box key. I doubted whatever other secrets Paula uncovered would prove whether Hiro had been a spy or not.

Mom had helped solve my last case. I clenched my jaw as I dialed her number.

"Don't tell me you finally picked a date," she said.

Whatever happened to the old *Hi, how are you* greeting? "I haven't. I will," I replied.

"You've been saying that since... Never mind. That is Russ's issue."

"And oddly, he isn't pushing me."

Mom chuckled, "That man is so much like your father sometimes."

My heart skipped a beat. No recrimination in her voice, just truth. "In what way?" I'd never really thought about Russ and my long-deceased dad as being similar.

"Your father had a way of gentle persuasion that could make the most hardened critics believe in something better."

That described Russ well. "It sounds like you admired him."

"I did. I'm sorry if you ever thought otherwise. I was completely lost without him."

I didn't remember it that way, but twenty years ago I'd been an angry teenager, blaming the person closest to me for fate.

"Well, you didn't call me to hash through that drama. I just spoke to your sister. She's fine. Isn't she?" Mom asked.

My overprotective mother at her best. Ever since my half-sister had decided to attend Bark U, I'd been in the line of fire. After her last adventure where she'd ended up a murder suspect, I guess I had to agree. "She's fine. I need your help with something else."

The crackle had to mean she'd dropped the phone. Was it that weird to ask your mom for help? Maybe for me.

"Sorry. I fainted," Mom said. "You really need my help?"

"If you can." I gave her the abridged version of Paula's quest.

"You think Hiro Tanaka was a spy?"

"Maybe. I don't know. It kind of makes sense."

73

"FRUPAC was in the old administration building at Pearl Harbor."

Sometimes she sounded like a naval officer herself. After thirty-something years as a Navy wife, I guess it made sense. "What does that mean?"

"Fleet Radio Unit Pacific. They were the cryptology group that broke the code that decided the Battle of Midway. It was also called Station HYPO. Look it up. Hiro Tanaka knew how the Japanese navy operated. His insight would've been invaluable to breaking the Japanese naval code."

I looked up the Battle of Midway on my phone. The timing fit. The Tanaka family had disappeared in December 1941. Could this be the missing piece? "Can you find out who served at HYPO?"

"I think so. I'll run over to Pearl in the morning. You know, eighty years is a long time to track someone who didn't want to be found."

I hated to think she might be right.

We talked for a few more minutes before Mom said, "It's way past your bedtime. I'll talk to you when I have something."

I stared at my cellphone screen. Had I just spoken to my mom for fifteen minutes without a single argument? Who said I couldn't change?

CHAPTER 11

Jack's high-pitched bark sliced right through me as he darted between my legs and into my townhouse. Sandy handed me a steaming cup of Woofing Best Coffee. No need to reprimand her Jack Russell Terrier; Winston took care of it. His snarl warned of serious sniffing repercussions.

I bit back a snarky comment, instead lacing my fingers around the warm paper cup. My first long swallow tempered my growl. I leaned against the doorframe and looked out over the sand. The winds had changed overnight, blowing the usual coastal fog out to sea and revealing that tropical paradise of rolling waves and blue sky we saw so infrequently. It was magical. No need for a sweatshirt: it had to be eighty degrees and so dry that my lips chapped. Man, I loved the warm easterly winds.

So did Sandy. She'd pulled her hair back in a smiley face scrunchie that matched her grin. We both wore blue, long-sleeved water shirts, board shorts and nonslip water shoes. I didn't intend to get wet, but... I looked at Winston oh-so-innocently wiggling his butt at my feet. Best to be prepared.

Russ showed up a few minutes later. Apparently, he'd gotten the fashion memo because he also wore a royal blue water shirt and board shorts. He towed a two-man dinghy outfitted with an electric motor on a boat dolly. So much for his faith in my paddling abilities. I thought about giving him a smile-down point but reconsidered after his explanation.

"The marine forecast says that it's blowing ten knots on the southwest-facing side of Bark Rock," he said. "I want to be prepared for those infamous gusts."

Russ, the ever diligent planner, got another smile-up point. I upped it to two points when he carried my paddleboard to the shoreline.

Smile up, 5. Smile down, 1.

Was it even a contest? I didn't bother to answer that question. I just needed to pick a wedding date—any date.

I clipped the bright orange doggie life vest Sandy handed me on Winston. He didn't fight me until I clipped on the neck float. Not that I blamed him. The Corgi's already-thick neck seemed stockier, but me sharing my normally solo board with a dog called for safety first. Mine, mostly, if I somehow lost this dog overboard.

Winston wasn't too constricted. After a few head shakes, he ran (or whatever that hopping Corgi run was called) as fast as Peter Cottontail, kicking up sand tuffs with every step until he splashed in the seawater. The dog swayed leg-deep in the surf until I caught up. He quickly exited and puppy-shook cold saltwater all over my sun-warmed clothing. Ugh!

I shrieked and jumped backward, bumping Sandy's paddleboard. She teetered from side to side. The attempted recovery really did it. Her feet tangled with Jack's, doing his normal figure eights between her legs. She stumbled to her knees. Jack rabbit-hopped to safety, yelping like a full-fledged tattletale.

Russ watched the whole thing from his dinghy and laughed. I didn't hear his merriment over the surf, but his tell-tale shoulder shake indicated his enjoyment. At least someone enjoyed it. There was nothing he could've done to help anyway.

I offered Sandy a hand up and apologized.

"It's not your fault." She glowered at Winston, who Corgi-smiled and planted his wiggle-butt on my paddleboard, ready to go.

"He didn't do it on purpose. He's just excited." His expressive ears bobbed, not missing a thing. Come on.

Sandy *hmm*ed. That she hadn't responded said something. He was a dog, not a chief strategist. I took a long look at the Corgi patiently seated on the nose of my board like an old-time figurehead. Obviously, Winston liked to ride. Maybe this wasn't a disaster looking to happen after all. One glanced at Russ, poised to follow, and I realized it didn't matter. He'd make sure we all came home safely today.

A vision of a little blonde girl with his blazing blue eyes splashing in the surf flashed in my mind's eye. The leopard-printed swimsuit had my name all over it. A warmth spread through me. Sandy was right. Embrace new things or be left behind—and I refused to do that.

On that thought, I took the big step onto the paddleboard and pushed off. I have to admit, Winston stood up like a champ. Through lapping waves, rolling surf, and splashing saltwater, he soldiered on like his Welsh forefathers. His short, stubby legs and low center of gravity made him a natural. In fact, I struggled in the choppy waves far more than he did. Jack, on the other hand, slid off the board with the poise of a frantically clawing cat, barking like a cornered Chihuahua. Russ fished him out of the ocean water half a dozen times before depositing him in the dingy, where the terrorist collapsed, his belly flat on the rubber bottom, hyperventilating.

Alone, Sandy kept pace despite the wind blowing across our boards until we slipped behind Bark Rock. The instant eye-of-the-storm calmness seemed surreal. No wind, no surf, no frolicking seagulls. Not even direct sunlight. Only the hum of the dinghy's electric engine as Russ made his way to the iconic rock's jagged edge.

Anticipation vibrated through Sandy and me as we swished through the now lake-calm water. Although I'd admired Bark Rock from shore for years, up close it seemed much larger and more imposing. It stood maybe twenty feet high and twice again as long. I suppose it could've been called a coastal island, since drought-resistant plants grew out of the many rock fissures and crevices, no doubted seeded by birds. The jagged walls possessed the same nook-and-cranny struc-ture found in the shoreline cliffs. On the southwest side, a rock pile about ten feet high extended thirty or so feet. The jagged stone chunks showed extensive weathering, indicating a long-ago rock slide. Just how tall had Bark Rock been eighty to a hundred years ago, before the many destructive earthquakes?

Russ beached the dinghy five feet from the rocks. Sandy and I followed, pulling our paddleboards onto the sandy incline. Could this have been Jonathan Douglas's secret beach back in 1920? I closed my eyes, visualized the elusive phoenix symbol, and then scanned the rocks, high to low, side to side. Not even a hint. No shadows or structure looked even close.

Had this all been a wild goose chase? Disappointment stirred until Russ opened a hardcover black suitcase he'd stashed under the center seat beside the life vests. The box looked familiar. In fact, I'd seen the ground-penetrating radar while investigating Jan Douglas's murder. Although she'd been hunting for the Douglas Diamond, it had nothing to do with her death. Construction companies used the GPR to locate wires, gas lines, and crawl spaces beneath concrete to avoid construction site mishaps. "Is that...?"

"A GP8000. I borrowed it from a friend of mine in case we found something worth exploring." Russ's kid-in-the-gaming-store grin always amused me.

"Not from anyone in Barkview, I hope." That kind of gossip promised a riot in this treasure-obsessed town.

"You hope correctly. No need for gossip to out us before we are ready." Russ removed a handheld device twice again the size of his hand. "This won't work if the cave is underwater, but if we can locate an entrance..."

He stepped closer to the rock and flipped on the device, the beeping drowning out further explanation. Sandy monitored the tablet-like receiver while Russ methodically moved the device across the jagged rocks. The images on the screen looked a lot like what you see on an underwater depth finder. Fortunately, Sandy seemed to know what the brightly colored lines all meant and instructed Russ to make direction changes.

Boredom settled in after a few minutes. My attention wandered to the rocks themselves. The size and scope of the crevices offered a plethora of worthy hiding places...for birds and sea creatures. Not a chance a full-grown human could fit.

My optimism at risk, it took me a second to realize Winston and Jack had vanished. A genetic herder partnered with a fox hunter free to explore hundreds of little nooks and crannies? My blood pressure spiked just thinking about the mischief those two could cause.

"Sandy, call Jack." I tried hard to temper my concern. Winston was my responsibility. If something happened to him...

"What? Why?" She blinked as she looked up from the colorful screen.

"The dogs have gone AWOL." I gestured around us.

Her wide-eyed alarm matched mine, likely for different reasons. "Jack. Come, Jack." The octave increased with each word.

No barking, just the ominous whistling wind, broke the silence. Sandy called Jack again. Not even a peep from Sir Barks-a-lot? This couldn't be good. "They didn't swim away. We'd see their life vests in the water. They're here somewhere," I said.

"Jack comes when I call him. Unless he can't hear me."

Or doesn't want to, I added silently. I didn't even try to pretend Winston listened to me. That dog had a will of his own.

"If they found a cave, they couldn't hear us," Sandy suggested

Except a dog's hearing was four times better than a human's. I'd done a report on that too.

Russ abandoned the GPR to lead the dog search. Bark Rock wasn't that big. How hard could it be to find them?

Not too difficult, it turned out. We found both dogs on the southern rock pile, herding a sea lion into a crevice. Tail wagging, Jack easily leaped from rock to rock and jumped into Sandy's outstretched arms, licking her chin. Ick! She squeezed Jack so tightly he yelped in protest.

I would've hugged Winston if I could have reached him. More like a tightrope than a trodden path for the stockier dog hampered by a protruding life vest. How had he gotten down there anyway?

With no direct path to the Corgi, a sea rescue seemed the most efficient. Russ headed back for a paddleboard. I imitated Paula and put my hands on my hips and shook my forefinger at Winston. The dog's ears drooped like a wilted flower. If he had a tail, it would be between his legs.

Winston pivoted and disappeared behind a rock, materializing beside me a few moments later, his big blue eyes beseeching. Of course, I forgave him. I also gave up a perfect opportunity to reinforce a lesson. Winston had found a tunnel. Nothing else made sense.

I waved to Russ as he paddled up a few minutes later, towing Sandy's paddleboard. "Winston found a tunnel," I announced.

I expected excitement, not thoughtful regard somewhere over my shoulder. Had he heard me? We'd been looking for a cave for six months. Could this be the infamous hiding place Jonathan Douglas had taken refuge in?

Finally, Russ said, "Cat, you need to see this."

His dead-dog-seriousness couldn't be good. I looked around. No uninvited visitors. No rogue waves. What? I swallowed hard as I followed Winston down the trail. I'd never have called the Corgi surefooted until I saw him easily negotiate the narrow path. Together we climbed onto Sandy's paddleboard.

"Look at the rock's angle." My eye followed the line traced by Russ's finger.

With a little imagination, the rock shape did look like a phoenix. OMG! Had we really found it?

"What time will the sun be in the optimal position?" Russ asked.

"According to what we uncovered, it should be just before sunset. I'm guessing between five and six tonight," I replied.

Russ pivoted on the paddleboard, the weight shift not affecting his balance at all. "That would put the light angle about there." He pointed toward the beach area we'd been investigating before the dogs' disappearance. I really wanted to be excited, but sand led to solid rock. There wasn't a promising opening to a secret cave in sight.

Were we finally getting closer to the Douglas Diamond, or was this just another dead end?

I paddled closer to the shore, causing Sandy's paddleboard to push up against the rocks with each ebb and flow of the sea. Winston crouched on the bow, his little legs quivering in excitement as he leaped into the water. The belly flop splashed water every which way before he swam the last five feet. I guess he really didn't need the life vest. The Corgi's butt did float. In fact, his fluffy rear end had to be a good inch above the water while his front paws paddled together as if he were digging in the water. I couldn't help but laugh. When the dog reached the rocks, he climbed ashore, shook off any excess water, and invited Russ and me to join him with a head nod.

We did. Sandy pulled up beside us in the dinghy, handed Russ an LED flashlight and anchored the paddleboards, securing our transport home. We went ashore, not without a bit of drama. It was sheer luck I didn't fall in, actually. Russ caught me just in time. Never one to complain about strong arms holding me tight, I thanked him with a no-nonsense kiss.

Together we followed the Corgi's fur trail to a sliver in the rocks, more like a fissure than a real opening and hardly bigger than a small foxhole. Sleek Jack fit in just fine. Broad Winston wiggled halfway in and paused. Was he stuck? He squiggled this way, then that, finally popping through in a fur cloud.

No way either Russ or I would get in there. He had no luck strong-arming a boulder aside either. We were so close. Furballs! I stepped aside to allow Russ to point his flashlight beam inside. "You were right about the rock slide. This looks relatively recent."

I wasn't sure how he could tell. The rocks appeared damp and weathered.

"The earthquakes in May?" I asked. We'd had a series of them, trying both human and canine patience alike. "Madame

Orr said an earthquake would reveal..." I sucked in my breath. Had we just found Jonathan Douglas's hideout? "But this is nowhere near where the phoenix symbol led."

"Unless the symbol marks another or the original entrance," Russ suggested.

I wanted to believe him and watched as he focused on the rocks—striations in the rocks, to be exact. When he removed a pocketknife and scraped the stone, I knew something wasn't adding up. "What did you find?"

"Wave-form scarring." Russ didn't look up from his task.

"What?" I looked over my shoulder, waiting for Sandy's explanation. Too bad she'd stayed with the watercrafts.

Russ took a picture with his phone. "These rocks didn't fall in an earthquake. Someone blew them."

Talk about a literal bomb. I swallowed. "You mean, like dynamite?"

He nodded. "A long time ago. Look at the weathering and the..."

The light-colored lines looked like rock wrinkles to me. What did I know about geology?

Russ pointed the flashlight beam through the narrow gap. "We found someone's hideout."

"Jonathan's?" I hardly dared ask. I wanted to believe it. It would mean the end of a century-long hunt and possibly the beginning of a Russian revolution, but something felt wrong, very wrong. Dynamite existed in 1925, but who would blow up a rumrunner?

"Not unless Jonathan had a SSTR-1 Suitcase Radio circa 1940," Russ replied.

I didn't bother to ask for an explanation. Instead, I ducked under his armpit. Better to see for myself. No joke. Amid the crumbled rocks and an overturned metal chair lay remnants of a recognizable portable high frequency transmitter and a bleached bone... I jerked back, Russ's solid chest blocking my escape. "Is that a s-skeleton?"

"Part of one, anyway." His nonchalance said something about his coolness under duress. We were talking about a dead body. "This could well be the Japanese intercept post Paula searched for."

I swallowed hard. His arms felt good around me and made the whole scene okay.

"That radio's transmission radius was only about three miles. The main submarine had to have been patrolling along the coast," Russ continued.

"How could the Navy, Coast Guard, and all the coastal lookout posts have missed that?" I asked. "Bark Rock is less than a mile off the main beach." It made no sense.

"Arrogance? Good intel? Could've been a lot of things. Including that the Japanese sent in the mini-subs at predetermined times. Radar was in its infancy in 1942."

"Didn't World War II submarines need to surface every few hours for air?" I'd done some internet research after reading Paula's notes.

Russ nodded. Even more reason they should've been discovered.

"Who manned this station? And why use dog couriers?" I asked.

"Whoever was here needed supplies. Someone in Barkview had to provide food and water in addition to information."

We kept circling back to a traitor in Barkview. I still couldn't believe it. Or maybe I just didn't want to.

"What's bothering you?" Russ asked.

"Where do I start?" Seriously, this whole quest was overwhelming—so many moving parts. I had a hard time keeping track of the details. "My biggest question is, why has no one found this cave in eighty years? It's not like Bark Rock is off-limits or anything."

"The recent earthquakes may have shifted the rocks just enough to reveal the opening. The inside appears well preserved for eight decades in the elements," Russ said. "If this was Jonathan's hideout..."

He saw my realization turn to dread. I couldn't verbalize the possibility.

Russ did. "It means the Japanese spy could have found the Douglas Diamond."

My heart sank to my toes. Could the diamond really have been found all those years ago? A shred of hope lit. "If the spy died in there, maybe the diamond is still there."

Russ's maybe didn't begin to sound convincing. "Or the spy bought loyalty with the stone."

"Meaning he traded it for his land support?" That would mean a Barkviewian had it all along. How could it remain hidden for so long?

"The police will need heavy equipment to get in there and find out."

Instant panic took hold. "Y-you can't report this..." Me, saying this to Mr. By-the-book? I rushed to explain. "Not until we find the Douglas Diamond." This wasn't an active murder investigation. The guy had been dead for eight decades. What would a few more days matter?

"I wouldn't dream of it. This is your quest," Russ said.

No hesitation meant I had a chance. I exhaled in pure relief. Russ's doing-the-right-thing could be inconvenient. I called Winston, who actually obeyed with butt-wiggling excitement. I expected to see his I'm-treat-worthy look, not the metal tube he dropped at my feet.

"That's the message tube Paula talked about. I'm sure of

it." I retrieved the pitted, silver cylinder and unscrewed the cap while Russ praised Winston.

Inside, an aged paper scroll seemed intact. No water damage or mildew. Only a faint yellowing, I realized, as I unrolled the sheet. The paragraph of gibberish meant nothing. The characters weren't Japanese, but English numbers and letters in no particular order. Did that mean the spy didn't write Japanese?

"It's a cipher," Russ said. "If I remember my history, the Japanese used several types for codes during World War II."

"Jordan told me about that. Can you read this?"

Russ gave Rodin's Thinker a run for his money, scratching his chin as he stared at the page. "Could be a simple letter replacement."

"Which means what?"

"If I had the key...." He crushed my enthusiasm. "It shouldn't be too difficult to break. They didn't have encryption supercomputers in 1942. Sandy and Jennifer should enjoy cracking it."

No doubt. I took a cell-phone photo. Both tech-savvy ladies would prefer an electronic version over paper anyway. I rerolled the coded message and stuffed it back in the tube, but something jammed in the bottom. I flipped over the tube and shook it. A metal disc on a simple chain clanked off the rocks. Dog tags? I scooped them up, knowing even before I read the name that they belonged to Lieutenant Junior Grade Henry Jones. So he really had existed. But how had it gotten here in a spy's communication tube? Unless...

"Could Henry Jones have been the spy?" I asked.

Russ scrutinized the dog tags. "We have someplace to look for information on Henry Jones now. I'll ask the chief to check with his contacts."

"What if he asks where you got the information?" I asked.

Russ's frown made me feel about two feet tall. I did trust him to keep his word. "Never mind."

Was this a simple case of wrong place at the wrong time for the unsuspecting visitor, or something more? More important, why had Charles Smythe covered up Henry Jones's hotel visit? Too many questions spun around in my head.

I took a deep breath. At the very least, the Jones family would get closure. I also now had all the pieces myself to find the Douglas Diamond. With any luck, in six hours, the phoenix would lead the way and fulfill a prophecy one-hundred-and-twenty years in the making.

Altruistic as it sounded, I didn't want to think about all the ramifications. I just craved closure.

CHAPTER 12

I arrived at the Barkview Bank just after lunch hour. The stately Victorian located on the corner of Third Street and Sycamore dated back to 1901. The pale yellow shake and gray-gabled building honored Barkview's rich past and promising future. Even Russ would approve of the state-of-the-art security system, which included electronic sensors and two take-you-down, fawn-colored Bullmastiffs named Brutus and Caesar. No missing those two sitting sphinx style in the marble entry. Weighing in at one hundred and thirty-plus pounds, the drooling muscle-machines might as well require horseshoes for their paws. Frankly, just thinking about picking up their daily poop pile made me nauseous.

"Good afternoon." I readjusted the brown leather messenger bag resting on my hip to protect my vital organs. Like that would stop those monster-dogs. Although I'd come a long way from running for cover every time I saw a scary big dog, they still upped my blood pressure.

"Good afternoon, Miss Wright." The bank's manager, Jesse James (not exactly an inspiring vote of financial confidence), met me at the glass door with a firm handshake. It didn't matter that my Aunt Char held a bank director's title. Jesse treated everyone with the same small-town warmth and attention. Dressed in a three-piece suit complete with an old-fashioned pocket watch dangling from his vest pocket, he could have been his predecessor performing the same task fifty years ago. Not that Jesse was that old. His salt-and-pepper hair and pale blue eyes just belonged to an old soul.

He looked behind me, no doubt for Winston, whom I'd left in the car with Sandy. Not because I doubted the dog's welcome—Barkview welcomed dogs everywhere—but because I couldn't dally. My intuition kept pointing me toward the past. That meant Sandy and Jennifer needed whatever Paula had deemed important enough to stash in the safe-deposit box before they started digging.

"Paula Powell left me the key to her safe-deposit box. I would like to access it."

Jesse nodded. "She confirmed your access over three months ago."

So Paula really had decided to turn this investigation over to me right after our interview. Good news or bad? Time would tell. Jesse motioned me to follow him. Decorated in rich woods and elegant stone, the bank definitely had an early-twentieth-century Boston vibe. "I am sorry to hear about Mrs. Powell. A fine woman."

I had to wonder what he'd think after this quest went public. We stopped for signature verification at the safe-deposit box desk. As if they couldn't identify me without my driver's license. I tempered my impatience; no point fighting this procedure. Once cleared, I trailed Jesse through the vault door into an area filled with endless rows of dark metal boxes in various shapes and sizes. One of the few original bank boxes still in use, the Barkview bank had added additional boxes in their new vault, but retained the older ones for their legacy customers.

I relinquished my key. Jesse confirmed the number and directed me to a midsize box, larger than most. "Ever wonder what's in some of these boxes?" My need-to-know motor kicked into high gear as I twisted my leopard-print scarf.

The same curiosity glittered in Jesse's gray eyes. "Although we've updated our boxes and security, some of our boxes haven't been accessed in well over fifty years."

That got my attention. "Sounds like some true Barkview time capsules," I remarked.

"I suppose they are. Providing the monthly fees are paid, the boxes remain active. I sometimes wonder if that which one generation deems valuable would hold the same importance to the current generation." Jesse inserted the bank's master key and then mine into the lock and slid the metal box from the wall. "This box is one of them. Until Paula added your name for box access, she hadn't opened it since 1948."

Which begged the question. "Wow! Who else has long-dormant boxes?"

"You know I can't disclose that information." Jesse winked. "I can say that a number of our multigenerational families do."

As I stood there surrounded by the antique metal, I pondered whether they held monumental treasure or a bygone era's junk. How many secrets were hidden away in those boxes, guarded through the generations in the name of tradition and family pride?

As if I'd let him stop there. "Any older than 1948?"

"Not that hasn't been accessed on a parent's death." Jesse's look begged for one more question.

Too bad his hint didn't resonate. Of course heirs accessed estate records. What was I missing? A vision of the Douglas Diamond in a dark box flashed before my eyes. No. That would confirm that a traitor had resided in Barkview. I refused to go there. The diamond had to be in the cave.

I followed Jesse to the well-appointed viewing room. "Let me know when you are ready to return the box to the vault," he said.

I nodded. The postage stamp–size room did have a black leather executive chair and cherry wood desk equipped with a high-magnification reading glass. No doubt to inspect documents. "Did Paula leave any messages for me?" It would be just like her.

Jesse smiled. At least, I think that slight lip raise represented a genuine smile. Relieved, he said, "Paula instructed me to tell you to look beneath the surface."

What did that cryptic clue mean? Trust Paula's clue to be as ambiguous as the quest itself.

I opened the lid the moment the door latched shut. Inside I found two leather-bound books, a letter, and miscellaneous notes.

I quickly tucked the contents into my briefcase and gestured to Jesse that I was ready to leave. Sandy, Jennifer, and I would look through this together.

I might as well have been a Hollywood Cold War spy, the way I looked over my shoulder as I crept in the Barkview Library's back door. With Sandy, Winston, and Jack bringing up the rear and my car parked in the adjacent lot, I doubted we achieved stealth. It just felt good.

Originally built with proceeds from Jonathan Douglas's bootlegging bounty, the three story, tan-shingled Victorian occupied a full city block that at one time enjoyed unobstructed Pacific Ocean views. Today, only a stroll along the top-story widow's walk offered a glimpse of the waves. Jonathan's granddaughter had converted the building into a library in the 1960s after a wildfire destroyed the town's original structure.

Jennifer Moore met us in the shadowed hallway, her twin ruby Cavalier King Charles Spaniels hugging her ankles. Gone was the conservative fortyish spinster, replaced by a fun-loving woman whose Spaniel-brown eyes danced with an inner mischief that went well with her stylish messy bun. The dark slacks and flowing floral print blouse she wore added a cheerfulness reflected in her step.

Winston shook his fluffy butt at the Cavaliers, while terrorist Jack went for a direct private parts sniff. Needless to say, the prissy Cavaliers ended that behavior. Their ensuing growls rivaled a Doberman's elocution. Jack's dive for protection tripped Sandy, sending her sprawling. Fortunately, Jennifer's quick reflexes saved Sandy from leveling the antique side table.

I watched the whole thing, doing my best not to laugh too hard. So, Winston wasn't the only tripping hazard. Maybe all small dogs were.

"Well, that was unexpected." No reprimand, just a head shake as Jennifer ushered us across the parquet floor and into the family-breakfast-room-turned-book-lined conference room. Except for a fancy multifunctional coffee machine, Eastlake elegance surrounded us. The green-striped chairs coordinated with period wallpaper around a highly polished oval table of English oak.

The current president of the Cavalier Crown Committee, which administered Barkview's annual Cavalier King Charles dog show, and the most efficient organizer I had ever encountered, Jennifer had turned our small-town library into a historical research destination in short order.

With Jack curled up in the corner and Winston crowding my space, I positioned two leather-bound books, a letter addressed to Paula's son, Charles Jr., and miscellaneous notes on lined paper on the table between their laptops.

"I can't believe Paula is dead. How...?" Jennifer's eyes misted. Paula had been a Barkview icon for so long, I expected similar reactions from just about everyone.

"We won't know until the autopsy is completed," I replied quickly, which was technically true. I shared a glance with Sandy. For Paula's granddaughter's sake, we needed to maintain Uncle G's call for secrecy.

Jennifer headed for the coffeemaker. "One caramel cappuccino for Cat. Sandy, what would you like?"

"Decaf mocha with cinnamon and a dash of nutmeg." Of course Sandy remembered Jennifer's coffee addiction. Who could forget? She'd named her precious dogs after the two spices.

The rich aroma of brewing Woofing Best Coffee wrapped its warmth around me. We would solve Paula's murder. Don't ask me how I knew. I just did.

I picked up the leather-bound book and flipped through the pages. "This book appears to list the Smythes' financial transactions from 1938 to 1946."

Sandy sorted the loose notes. "Here are instructions in Paula's handwriting that say a forensic accountant will verify government fraud."

"Paula has a record of Aaron Smythe defrauding the US government during wartime?" Coffee sloshed over the rim of Jennifer's coffee cup as she slid into the spindle chair beside me.

"I'm no accountant, but..." I handed Jennifer the book filled with columns of dates and figures associated with job descriptions. "This can't matter. The statute of limitations must've expired fifty years ago."

"That's not the point. Criminal activity undermines the Smythes' position in Barkview," Jennifer insisted. A pair of rose-gold-rimmed reading glasses appeared on her nose. Odd, I didn't know she even wore glasses.

"That was eighty years ago. Who cares?" I asked. Seriously, with no legal recourse and the perpetrator long buried, who cared?

"The court of public opinion." Clearly, it mattered to Jennifer. Did she represent Barkview's majority? If so, Adam Smythe's congressional campaign could be in jeopardy.

Jennifer waved one of the lined pages. "This is a list of the coastal lookout locations built by Smythe's company, with circled and diagrammed beach landing blind spots. I recognize Paula's handwriting on the back."

More like Paula's scrawl, but recognizable nonetheless. "It says it's from a decoded enemy radio transmission on February 26, 1942."

Winston's head popped up at the exact same time my intuition pinged. Had he felt it too? "That is the day Henry Jones disappeared."

"That can't be a coincidence." Sandy's eyes glittered like two-carat sapphires. I had to agree. "But does it incriminate Aaron or Charles Smythe? Charles tampered with Jones's hotel information."

"That is the question," Sandy said.

Jennifer just looked lost until I filled her in on Will's information about Charles's interference at the Old Barkview Inn.

Jennifer sucked in her breath. "No wonder Paula kept this information hidden. Her husband and the father of her son could well have been a traitor."

That Paula had been married to Charles Smythe still seemed odd. Even more so when Sandy opened the envelope addressed to Paula's son, Charles Jr. "It's from Charles, dated July 10, 1945, and postmarked from San Francisco to be opened on Charles Jr.'s eighteenth birthday."

My son. You are reading this because my responsibilities have kept me from watching you grow into the man I know your mother insisted you become. Heed her counsel as you take your rightful place as head of the family. Your mother is the strongest and most ethical person I know. I implore you to do what is right without thought to personal cost and to carry out your duty with pride. Know that you are loved.

Forgive my weakness. I am confident you are a better man than I.

Your loving father.

"Geez! That's a mountain of guilt for an eighteen-year-old kid." Sandy nailed that one.

The letter did read like a father's farewell to his son that needed to get by a military censor, but something about the wording struck me as odd. Paula's warning to look beneath the surface came to mind. "When did Charles die?" I knew he didn't return from the war.

Jennifer referred to her computer. "He was killed on July 30, 1945, when a Japanese submarine torpedoed the USS *Indianapolis* en route from Guam to the Philippines."

"Twenty days after he wrote the letter?" I asked. "July 10 had to be his last day in port."

"Talk about bad luck. I mean, the war in the Pacific had all but been won by then," Sandy added.

"There's more," Jennifer said. "The USS *Indianapolis* carried the parts for the atom bomb destined to destroy Hiroshima and Nagasaki."

We all thought the same thing, I could tell. Was the ship's sinking more than a tragic accident? Charles had worked in radio intercept; why would he be on that boat?

"I remember seeing his headstone in the Barkview Cemetery," Sandy said. "How did the Navy send his body back?"

Jennifer's long silence bothered me. "They didn't. The USS *Indianapolis* debacle was a naval cluster."

Strong words from Jennifer, for sure. I knew why when she continued.

"More sailors died waiting to be rescued in the shark-infested waters than actually went down on the ship. The Navy listed Charles as missing in action until a surviving sailor brought Aaron Smythe Charles's dog tags and told him how his son heroically went down with the ship evacuating men. Eventually, the Navy reclassified him as buried at sea and gave him a medal of valor. Aaron Smythe commissioned the headstone in the family plot."

"Is that why Paula waited seven years to remarry?" Sandy asked.

A good question. Paula would never chance committing bigamy.

Sandy interrupted my musings with a shout. "You're not going to believe what this is." She waved the second tan leather book.

Judging from her surprise, I was afraid to ask. Winston's sudden snore gave me another minute to decide whether I really wanted to know. "What?"

"It's a handwritten list of the Old Barkview Inn's guest registry from December 1941 to 1945." Sandy flipped through the pages. "Henry Jones is listed here. There's a question mark beside his name. There are quite a few question marks."

"Why would Paula have that information?" Jennifer's brow knitted as she scanned the names. Suddenly, she sat straighter, if that was even possible, and typed something into the keyboard. "Aha! Da bomb."

The first key stroke got our attention. The 1990s jargon stopped time. "This is a list of Nazi sympathizers," Jennifer announced. "I recognized a few names from a novel I just read."

"You have time to read for fun?" How did she do it? I collapsed when I left the office. Jennifer managed two flourishing organizations.

"It's what I do to relax," she replied. "You play pickleball or chase mysteries."

True. I returned to topic. "The spies were staying at the Old Barkview Inn during the first months of World War II?" I couldn't believe it. Our iconic hotel a haven for spies?

"Our very own Palácio Estoril. I can see Ian Fleming in his panama hat hanging at the Terrace Bar, savoring a martini shaken, not stirred."

The James Bond reference suddenly made sense, as did Jennifer's dreamy look. For once, Sandy needed an explanation that I could supply. "Since Portugal remained neutral during World War II, Lisbon was full of spies and misinformation. Ian Fleming supposedly drew his inspiration for the James Bond books from his stay there."

"Oh. The real-life Daniel Craig," Sandy said.

I'd half-hoped for an Avengers reference.

Jennifer's half smile seemed suggestive. "Of course, you mean Pierce Brosnan."

Sandy's look pleaded for help before she sought refuge behind her computer screen. I should've just let it go, but ... "You mean Roger Moore." My father and Aunt Char had grown up on Sean Connery and Roger Moore and indoctrinated me into the Bond cult as well. To this day, I see every Bond movie on opening night.

"You can't be serious." Jennifer's crossed arms promised a heated argument, no doubt backed up with fanatical detail.

I was ready, but one look at the time, and I knew retreat was the better part of valor. "I think our Bond discussion needs to be revisited later. The important point is, why the Old Barkview Inn?"

"I think I know," Sandy interjected. "An Italian family bought the hotel in 1933."

"Were they fascist sympathizers?" It made sense. Italy under Mussolini had aligned with Germany and Japan.

"Family name Contiano," Sandy said.

"Conti." I'd learned too much about that family in a previous adventure. Best to focus on the goal. "Is there anything on Miyo Tanaka?" So many events started with her.

Sandy and Jennifer traded looks.

"What?" I asked. "I have a feeling." Okay, I admitted it.

They groaned in unison. Talk about a confidence threat. "Come on. Miyo has to be the missing link that ties this all together. Nothing else makes sense."

"Hold that thought." Sandy sorted through the notes. "The only reference I've found to Miyo is Paula's note dated August 1942. The sighting was at Pearl Harbor Naval Headquarters by a local source Paula could not verify. The bottom of the note mentions there was no census or military confirmation."

Could the Tanakas have changed their names? But why? How did the family even get to Hawaii after Pearl Harbor? In those days, there were no daily nonstop flights.

Jennifer tapped on her keyboard. "The last record of Hiro Tanaka was the FBI arrest reported in the *Bark View*. The Tanaka family vanished a few weeks later. No internment order was issued for transport for the family. Did the government even know they existed?"

"Which means what, exactly?" I had to ask.

"Anything and everything," Sandy chimed in. "We'll start looking."

I nodded. So many unanswered questions. I wondered if answers were even findable so many years later. I needed to check in with Uncle G. Maybe he'd been able to connect the dots on Hiro Tanaka.

"Russ and I found something at Bark Rock I need you two to look at. I'm sending it to your phone," I said.

Sandy's phone beeped. Her expression rivaled a kid's at the amusement park. "You found something in the cave?"

"Jonathan Douglas's cave?" Jennifer asked.

Pin-dropping silence filled the room. Even the dogs quit snoring. "It wasn't Jonathan Douglas's. We think it might have been a World War II signal station."

"You mean there really was a Japanese traitor?" Sandy asked.

"I don't believe it." Jennifer sounded just like Paula.

"It's a coded message. Can you break it?" I asked her. "Russ thinks it might be a substitution cipher. Whatever the note says may be what we need to find the intended recipient."

I hated to leave, but the two techno-brainiacs didn't need my help to solve a puzzle. "I need to talk to Madame Orr before tonight's adventure."

"Looking for the Douglas Diamond?" Jennifer asked, too casually. I must've blushed because her grin widened.

"Just another Friday night in Barkview," I said. For me and everyone else in town.

CHAPTER 13

A calm-before-the-storm peace settled over me as I parked in front of the yellow-and-white-gabled Victorian housing Madame Orr's psychic reading room. Even the swishing curtain above the wildflowers and variegated coleus didn't affect my blood pressure today. I would've been disappointed if Madame Orr hadn't been expecting me.

Although time had mellowed many of my not-so-flattering predispositions regarding fortune-tellers, I still did not trust her. How could I when her family's claim to the Douglas Diamond could change history as we know it?

Winston blocked my path through the bright yellow door, sniffing warily. Granted, this place had an unsettling vibe, but the dog needed to follow my lead. I tried to step over him, but the Corgi's block-and-tackle move sent me sprawling into the rich agarwood-scented parlor. How had I not cleared his two-foot-high back? I wondered as my shoulder connected with the round, café-sized wood table just before bouncing on the wood floor. Ouch! I was going to feel that in the morning.

I massaged my abused shoulder and pulled myself to

standing with the help of a beige upholstered wing-back chair. Out of the corner of my eye, I saw the deck of oversized celestial tarot cards on the tabletop and gulped. Not the way I wanted to start this conversation.

Madame Orr specialized in putting people off their game. I needed answers today. I couldn't let her get under my skin. Dressed in her usual shimmering, flowing robe, the large-boned woman seemed to float like an apparition across the area rug. "Yet another new friend, Catalina. Will you ever accept your match?" Her singsong voice certainly fit her colorful persona.

I just inclined my head. The contrast of her plaited black hair with her pale skin always held my eye.

Winston, his neck hair puffed like the mane of a lion on alert, scooted between us, feet sturdy and teeth bared. A Corgi bodyguard? I choked on a laugh. Was he protecting me from Madame Orr or her I-couldn't-believe-it-wasn't-a-lamb Bedlington Terrier, Danior? With filbert-shaped ears and a pear-shaped head, the plush toy de-squeaker looked like he was foaming at the mouth because of the white toy stuffing clinging to his snout. The dog's low-pitched growl didn't help any either.

Ugh! A dogfight I did not need. I stepped over the Corgi. Winston growled and brushed by my ankles, separating us again. I gaped at my midget defender. "Winston, stay." I stepped over him again. The dog ignored me and repositioned himself. The clash of wills continued.

It didn't take a psychic to see this wasn't going to end well. Madame Orr ended the standoff. She shooed Danior into another room and closed the door. Winston huffed and sat warily at my side.

Had I just been tested? A history between Paula and Madame Orr suddenly seemed all too possible. Did it matter?

Before I could go down that rabbit hole, Madame Orr changed the subject. "Tonight is a Santa Ana wind." The glint in her heavily charcoaled, dark-as-night eyes challenged me to disagree.

No need to. I repeated her prophecy. "'On the eve of the east wind, the golden sun will rise from the shifting sands.' I've come for further guidance. But you know that."

"A reading?" Her rounded shoulders straightened.

"Advice," I said quickly. I hadn't come that far.

Her chuckle lightened the mood. "As you wish." She motioned for me to sit across the table from her. The aroma of my go-to caramel cappuccino wafted from the mug to my right. Maybe someone anticipating my needs had benefits. I sipped the hot liquid as I waited for Madame Orr to complete her ritual deep breathing and settle in.

"The rising sun brings danger to those who seek it."

I'd half expected her first words to spike my heart rate, but not a way-too-close-to-home comment. Again begging the question, was she really a talented psychic or just possessed of an intuition that rivaled my own?

She didn't define the danger. Was she referring to the World War II Japanese spy or to sunrise over the Pacific being the optimal time to locate the Douglas Diamond? Too many possibilities came to mind.

I needed clarity and used her words intentionally. "Is the Douglas Diamond ready to reveal itself?"

Madame Orr took a deep breath. An odd stillness seemed to settle around her. "I've lost my connection to the diamond."

I blinked. I couldn't help myself. Talk about a bombshell admission from the self-proclaimed Douglas Diamond guru. "Has someone already found it?"

Her head shake caused her gold chandelier earrings to

tinkle. "I don't know. My time in Barkview is coming to an end, but I don't see the diamond."

I believed her. The pained look in her eyes said way too much.

"I have always thought it would be you who would start the cycle," she added almost regretfully.

A rug-pulled-from-beneath-you moment for sure. Deep down, I'd hoped so too.

Madame Orr must've read my disappointment because she hurriedly added, "Your destiny lies elsewhere now."

"Elsewhere?" What did that mean? I really hated the psychic mumbo jumbo.

Her many neck chains glittered in the lamplight as she nodded. "I know you don't believe in destiny."

I suppose in a way I did. Cold, hard facts only told part of the story. They rarely explained how the choices leading up to the event occurred. "Do you see Chad?" That Madame Orr had been the internet blogger's spiritual advisor still bothered me. Not Madame Orr's involvement, exactly, but that a true man of science used what amounted to the dark arts to further his fame.

"Chad will decide what is important in due time." Her certainty helped. "With a little help."

I really wanted to ignore her inference, as if I controlled Chad Williams's ego. "Do you have any last advice for me?"

"Heed your father's teachings, for he has given you much from the grave. Perhaps life's most important lessons are realized only when faced with an untenable choice," she said.

Ugh! Of course I wanted more clarity, but she wasn't offering any. Her words stirred up too many painful thoughts better left in my past. My father had been killed in action twenty-one years ago. What wisdom could he have bestowed on an adolescent that would matter now? I thought about

Charles Smythe's letter to his son. Had his words shaped Charles Jr.'s choices?

Tears threatened as the yellow door closed firmly behind me. I would never see Madame Orr again, I realized. No one would. Whatever happened next with the Douglas Diamond, Natasha Anna Roma Koratova would take her rightful place beside her wannabe king nephew and fulfill her destiny. Barkview's psychic was finally going home.

CHAPTER 14

My stomach growled as I parked at police headquarters. Winston noticed too. I could tell by the way he licked his chops. We'd both missed lunch. A quick visit to the Sit and Stay Café to pick up a burger bribe for Uncle G couldn't hurt, nor would getting the "take" on Paula's death from the third generation owner, Nell Witman. After Madame Orr's revelation about the rising sun, my intuition again pointed me toward the Tanaka family. Nell might have some insight on that too.

The walk from police headquarters to the quaint 1920s green-gabled Craftsman bungalow should've taken five minutes or less. It was basically right next door. Of course, Winston's sniff-a-thon slowed me down. For a dog who reportedly craved exercise, why did he lift his leg on every tree trunk, light post, and mailbox?

By the time we arrived at the Sit and Stay Café's wraparound veranda, the crowd spilled into the garden of well-tended seasonal daisies and colorful mums.

In all fairness, the twenty people milling about waiting to

be seated weren't the problem. The dogs blocking the aisle were. For efficiency, I tried to pick up Winston, but he wasn't having any of it; instead, he extra wiggle-wiggled his butt past a lip-smacking Newfoundland.

I squeezed around a standard Poodle, missed two Dachshunds by a heel, and barely avoided a Golden Retriever collision en route to the reception desk. There Nell directed traffic with her usual angelic calm.

"So it's true. Your journey continues," she stated.

Ugh! I could kill Ariana, Barkview's jeweler, for coining that phrase. My dog-sitting duty really had to be a cosmic joke.

Nell skirted the podium, quickly scratched Winston's ears, sending Corgi glitter airborne, and threw her arms around my neck. Dark haired and diplomatic with a look-alike black lab companion, she had frequently offered me level-headed and business-savvy advice. Lately, my schedule seemed to have less time for our ritual Kahlua and coffee discussions. Forget Nell's schedule. Between running two successful Barkview businesses, captaining a nationally ranked flyball team, and volunteering for an insane number of canine charities, I wondered when she slept. My perceived stresses really paled in comparison.

"Yeah!" What else could I say? I returned her hug while Winston and Nell's black lab, Blur, exchanged sniffs.

"I see we do need to catch up." I couldn't resist Nell's smile. "But today I need bribes for Uncle G and for you to deliver lunch to Sandy and Jennifer at the library."

"And a salad and a French fry or two for you." Nell typed my order into the computer without looking up. Was I really that predictable?

Winston's ankle nudge about knocked me over. I swear that dog understood when he'd been left out. "And a bone for Winston," I added quickly.

Nell paused. "He prefers a hotdog with extra mayo."

"Ick." Nell's shoulder-length hair bobbled as she laughed. Everyone knew hot dogs made me green and it wasn't the dog part. A childhood ER visit had left a lasting impression.

I shot the evil eye at Winston. Not even a stutter step. The dog stood his ground. In fact, he cocked his Corgi head to the right and gave me the I'm-worth-it grin that just made me laugh. "Fine," I said.

At least Nell waited for my acquiescence before sending my order. "Rumor has it you've been sniffing around Bark Rock for the diamond."

Her revelation had my full attention. So much for our attempted stealth. Apparently, no one bought the Corgi paddleboard adventure. How else could the Barkview gossip superhighway have gotten the scoop so quickly? More importantly, had it been a mistake not to call in the police to investigate the skeleton cave right away? If someone stumbled on it and wrecked the crime scene—if there was a crime scene—I'd be at fault. "I guess that's a better excuse than getting caught in the current," I said loud enough for the curious eavesdroppers to overhear.

"That's your story?" Nell wasn't buying it, but I knew she'd keep my secret.

"And I'm sticking to it."

Nell laughed out loud. "I bet Winston came to your rescue."

The Corgi's expressive ears seemed to vibrate in agreement. How did I know that? Was I starting to get this dog? "Uh, yeah. He's an amazing swimmer."

"You mean you fell in?" Amusement replaced pity in a blink.

Wrong tactic on my part. I swear I felt every eye in the place on me. Better they fixate on my inabilities than the real reason. Of course, I blushed. "Tandem isn't exactly my thing."

Winston took issue with that comment. He shook his butt and rubbed against my leg.

"Well, it looks like Winston is willing to try again." Nell crouched and scratched his head again. Now I got that cue. My knees creaked as I knelt beside her to scratch the dog and hear her for-my-ears-only whisper. "I figured the little expedition had something to do with Paula's death."

"Why would you think that?" I asked.

Nell's look had subterfuge written all over it. "I heard you left her house with an envelope yesterday. I figured she turned over her eighty-year-old witch hunt to you."

"You know about Paula's quest?" Was I the only one who hadn't known?

"Kind of. My great-aunt was Charles Smythe Jr.'s secretary back in the 1960s. She replaced Paula."

"Paula was CJ's secretary?" That explained how Paula had gathered sensitive information on Aaron Smythe. "Was your great-aunt friends with Paula?"

Nell shrugged. "My mother said the two women were kindred souls. Both too moral for an imperfect world."

That sounded like the Paula I knew. I waited for Nell's revelation. It was coming. I felt it.

"The important part is that my great-aunt married a Conti in 1969."

"The tangled web we weave." What else could I say? Nell had more to share. I could tell.

Nell's smile broadened. "True. Her father-in-law was awarded the Medal of Freedom by the Secretary of the Navy for meritorious service during World War II."

"For what?"

"I don't know. It had to be good, though. He owned the Old Barkview Inn until 1970-something."

A task for Sandy and Jennifer, for sure. Nell handed me the

take-out bags. "I added a meatloaf sandwich for Russ. He just called in a pickup order. Figured you'd want to deliver it personally." Her wink made me blush. "I'll see what I can do about quelling the Douglas Diamond gossip. I wish you'd find it already. The suspense is killing us all."

Me too. I didn't want to believe Madame Orr's latest prediction. I wanted to find it.

"Any more thoughts on the wedding date?" Nell's question failed as an afterthought. I heard no pressure in her question, just an I'm-getting-too-old-for-this-patience erosion. I ground my teeth. "Never mind. You'll figure it out eventually."

Russ had said the same thing. Was I that obviously conflicted? Any decision had to be better than this.

I thanked Nell and pointed Winston toward police head-quarters. We met Russ on the sidewalk about halfway. He kissed my cheek, scratched Winston, and promptly sneezed before relieving me of the bulging Sit and Stay Café carry out bags. That I hadn't even surprised him a little bothered me. It's not every day I drop everything and bring him lunch. Unless... "Did Nell tell you I was coming?"

"No."

All innocence, I believed him. "Then how did you know?" Was he tracking my phone? Did he have someone watching me? I squelched that paranoid thought. Invading my privacy wasn't Russ's style. Someone had told him.

My narrowed, contemplative gaze gave me away.

"I will not reveal my sources." A speculative smile broke through his seriousness.

Sure, I'd pulled the same line on him, but I really was, at heart, an investigative reporter. Which, by definition, meant I could figure it out on my own. I pictured the café, mentally assessing and disregarding suspects. The informant had to have been there. No officers or station employees had been inside. Hmm. Problem was everyone knew everyone. Was it even possible to have secrets in this town? But people did. Too many of them, in fact.

Russ held the door for Winston and me to enter. I led the way to Uncle G's office, where Max and Maxine sat at attention, flanking Uncle G, who rose from behind his cavernous desk. Both dogs thanked me for the treats with a shake of their elegant German Shepherd heads, sending globs of silver fur airborne in the filtered light. Oddly, Russ rarely sneezed around the deputies. Yet, with Winston, the man's allergies exploded. Russ fed Winston the hot dog before biting into his sandwich. Uncle G scratched his beard as I stole one French fry from his stash before handing over the burger bag. The aroma of freshly grilled beef teased my taste buds. "I was just about to call you," he said after two satisfied bites.

"Good news?" I paused, my fork mid-stab into my boring grilled chicken salad. Why did "being good" mean tasteless?

"You owe me for this one." His raised brow indicated a burger didn't begin to pay off this debt.

"Add it to my tab." This open-ended favor thing really chafed. Knowing Uncle G, his payback would make the national debt seem less daunting. "What do you have?"

"First, the Lieutenant Henry Jones you asked about mustered out of the Navy in 1945."

"You're sure?"

"Of course I'm sure. Military records do not lie."

People do. I suppose the dog tags could have been lost. With any luck, Sandy could find something more.

"Second." Uncle G took another bite of his burger, prolonging my wait.

This had to be good. He rarely went for a drum roll without cause.

"Hiro Tanaka was not picked up by the FBI. ONI activated him."

If he expected a wow, I disappointed him. I worked in TV. Government acronyms required explanation.

Russ filled in the blanks. "That's the Office of Naval Intelligence."

Uncle G added, "Tanaka's Imperial Navy experience made him a perfect recruit."

"To be a spy?" Of course. My pulse jumped. We were getting closer. I could feel it. Why, then, did every answer stir up more questions? "Paula said Hiro served on an early aircraft carrier. How could that help? The carriers had to have changed in the ten years since he came to the US."

"Hiro understood Navy protocols and terminology," Russ said.

Like that explained anything.

Uncle G referred to his notes. "ONI apparently thought it mattered. They sent him on a mission to Okinawa in 1944. I don't have details. He never returned."

"You mean he's still MIA?" I knew that acronym.

"As far as we know. World War II records are not always complete. Ships sank, beaches were destroyed. Dog tags are still found in unlikely places," Uncle G said.

I shared a glance with Russ. No kidding. We'd found dog tags in an obscure California rock. "What did Hiro do from 1942 to 1944?" I asked.

Uncle G shook his head. "No record."

Great. More secrets likely buried eighty years ago. "Did the ONI protect the rest of the family?" That would explain a lot.

"There was no protective custody back then," Uncle G said.

"They were also of Japanese descent," Russ added.

Hard to hide them with all mainland Japanese sent to internment camps. "Could they have gone to Hawaii?" Paula's

111

single Miyo sighting came to mind. It would've been easier to blend in there, live a life of sorts.

"There is no record of Hiro being n Hawaii after 1933."

The timeline's holes bothered him too. What had Hiro been doing? Where had his family disappeared to? Had Miyo just been another casualty of World War II? Her importance felt even stronger to me now. Without finding her, I'd never complete Paula's quest.

I rose to leave. Maybe my mother had news. A year ago I'd have laughed if someone told me I'd even be talking to my mother, never mind relying on her for information.

Uncle G stopped my quick departure. "Rumor has it you two are going after the Douglas Diamond tonight."

"We are." Russ's smooth reply avoided a need to come up with a dodge.

Uncle G stroked crumbs off his bread. "You think Bark Rock is the real location?"

If he'd heard the gossip, everyone had. Good or bad, the secret was out. Which meant every treasure hunter in the know would be there. Did I dare chance someone stumbling on the cave?

I glanced at Russ. He'd committed to silence. The decision was mine. I'd almost convinced myself to let it ride until Winston barked—a single, guilt inducing reprimand that pushed me over the top.

"We found a cave." I blurted out the words ready for a lecture.

Russ folded his arms and smiled as if he'd known I'd tell all in the end. Was he rubbing off on me?

Uncle G sat back in his chair. "So, you found the diamond?"

"Not exactly." I started to tell the tale, but Russ took over when I mentioned the bone.

Oddly, the chief didn't interrupt. He just stroked his chin, a fresh toothpick spinning like a top, listening. "Just so I'm clear, the bones could belong to Jonathan Douglas or a World War II radio operator?"

Verbalized, the hypothesis sounded crazy. Russ's nod helped. No argument from Uncle G. His toothpick just snapped. "I'll alert the forensic anthropologist. We'll need to confirm the age of the bones before we can start an investigation. Bark Rock is under my jurisdiction."

"A jackhammer and generator should get us inside quickly," Russ said.

"Providing the rock doesn't collapse." Uncle G typed something into his phone. It pinged a moment later. "We will assemble at Lifeguard Tower One in an hour."

"Better bring scuba gear," Russ added.

"I'm coming," I piped in. "And Sandy. She's earned her place." Winston's bark indicated he was coming too.

The chief glared at the Corgi. Had to admire the dog's tenacity. He stared back until Uncle G grumbled. "I'll have the boys block off the backside of Bark Rock now. It's time to find that diamond. This town needs closure."

Not only the town, I realized. Maybe Madame Orr was right. It didn't matter who found the diamond. The hunt just needed to be over.

CHAPTER 15

Surprised and relieved that Uncle G agreed to civilian participation, I knew any delay on my part would not be tolerated. Anticipation tempered by an odd hesitancy seemed to hang over me as I drove north on First Street toward home. I had just enough time to change into water-friendly clothing for this evening's adventure. Maybe it was the telltale red-orange sky I'd waited so long for shimmering over the Pacific. Sure, I'd always envisioned myself holding the Douglas Diamond, but I didn't crave the glory. I really just wanted closure. With Uncle G heading this expedition, I'd be lucky to get a photo for my story.

I saw Chad Williams's candy-apple-red Jeep Wrangler following behind a GMC truck in my rearview mirror. Coincidence? My intuition said no. If he'd heard the Bark Rock gossip, he likely either wanted to grill me on specifics or be part of the expedition. Not that I blamed him. He'd been hunting for the diamond longer than I had. Still. Why not just call and ask?

Before I could dial his number myself, my mother's phone number flashed on my phone screen.

"You aren't going to believe this." Mom's no-nonsense tone spilled through my car speakers.

My eagerness notched up. "Okay. Let's hear it."

"It turns out that code-breaking unit I told you about..."

"Station HYPO at Pearl Harbor." Too cool a name to forget.

"Yes. Well, they were pretty important to the World War II war effort. They worked in a vault in the basement of the administration building called the Dungeon. Records show that the team members were all white men. The officer in charge was LCDR—sorry, Lieutenant Commander—Joe Rochefort. He spoke Japanese fluently. The important thing is that their numerous linguists worked there. The group decoded JN-25. That was the Japanese naval code and estab-lished the Japanese Imperial Fleet organizational and command control structure." Mom's voice seemed to build into a crescendo. Even Winston felt it. He stood and gave me that Corgi smile. I scratched his ears with my free hand.

"Isn't that what intelligence does?" I was missing something.

"Yes, but think about this. You grew up in the military and don't understand what you so fondly call 'Navy talk.'"

"True. The acronyms make me crazy."

"The Japanese navy's terminology wasn't the same as ours," Mom replied.

My pulse leaped. "You're saying..."

"That team needed inside information..."

"And you think..." Did I dare hope?

"I'd bet my Imperial Oolong on it."

I whistled. A crazy tea lover, Mom wagering the equivalent to my Woofing Best Coffee meant a sure thing. "Why?"

"Mac Showers, one of the HYPO team members, sketched out the floor plan of the working area in 1942 for a commemo-ration of the contribution of intelligence to the war effort. I'll text it to you. There is one unlabeled desk in the center of the drawing at the bottom. The Navy historian told me that there was a rumor of a small-statured man a Navy car dropped off at Naval Headquarters daily. No one knew where he went, but he seemed to disappear into the basement."

It made sense. "Are there any descriptions of the mystery man?" Curiosity had to have gotten to someone.

"The only description the historian found was that he wore Navy-issue khakis and a plantation hat," Mom replied.

Her pause worked. I got it. "Not regulation." A must in wartime.

"Not Hawaiian civvy attire either."

Only someone who didn't want to be recognized would wear that wide-brimmed hat. "Why would the Station HYPO team keep a Japanese intelligence guy quiet after all these years?"

"They all took a secrecy oath."

Like that explained it. To a career military wife who'd also been married to a Navy Seal, I guess it did. Me? Not so much.

"Perhaps Tanaka didn't want his role to be known. He did sell out his country. That would make him a target for sympathetic Japanese," Mom pointed out. "Also, anti-Japanese sentiment ran high following Pearl Harbor. He could've just been cautious."

He did have a family to protect. "Can you find out more about this mystery man?"

"I can try. You do realize that 158,000 Japanese and 100,000 military personnel lived in Hawaii during World War II," Mom said.

No easy task. "You can limit the search to a family that included a man, a woman, and two daughters." How many could there be, with all the men enlisting?

Mom's laugh came out as a snort. "You do realize that the

Japanese weren't allowed to enlist until 1943. And this mystery man likely didn't want to be found."

I got it. "They couldn't have lived that far from Pearl Harbor. The H-1 freeway didn't exist. Island travel wasn't easy."

"Hawaii was under martial law from December 1941 to October 1944. Housing was in short supply. I'll do some research, but the military could've stashed a high-value family anywhere. The most relevant census would've been in 1950."

"They had to settle somewhere after the war," I said.

I heard her we're-searching-for-the-proverbial-needle-in-a-haystack warning. I needed more specific information to narrow the search area. Had we really found Hiro Tanaka and his family, or was this just an unprovable theory?

"Something else I found in the Coast Guard files might interest you. In January and February 1942, the Coast Guard patrols doubled off the Barkview coast."

"Were they looking for something?"

"Maybe. The interesting thing is that no boat was ever found, but a badly battered body was. The coroner's report said it had been hit by a boat. The body was identified as Haruto Yamaguchi, from a jade family ring that miraculously survived on his left hand," Mom explained. "It was ruled an accident. I'll send you a copy of the report."

Mom had read my mind. Sandy had told me about Haruto, but the timing bothered me. A Japanese man drowned at the same time another man went missing? And the body could only be identified by a ring? My intuition screamed foul.

I thanked Mom for her help. Her sleuthing skills were admirable. As I changed lanes to continue north on First Street, Chad pulled in right behind me. No doubt about it—he wanted to talk. Winston either sensed or saw him too. The dog crouched in a ready-to-defend posture. I tried not to laugh. Watch out, ankles.

No sense pulling over and causing a Barkview incident. He seemed intent on following me home anyway. I instructed my car to call Sandy and invited her to join this afternoon's expedition.

"Cool. I'll drop off Jack and head right down."

Had to love her enthusiasm.

"Just so you know, Chad Williams is following me home right now. He must've heard about our expedition."

"No doubt. I hear his mother isn't doing well. Her medical bills have to be piling up. I heard there was a medical trial he was trying to get her into, but no luck so far," Sandy said.

Trust Sandy to know all the gossip. "Maybe Aunt Char can make a call and help."

"I figured you'd say that. Specifics are on your phone." Indignation snuck into Sandy's voice as she changed subjects. "You aren't going to believe some of the shady stuff going on in Barkview back in the 1940s. Aaron Smythe Sr. should've been slammed." Her afternoon of research had paid off.

I had a pretty good idea what Sandy had discovered, but I let her vent. "He flat-out stole land and businesses from Japanese Americans. Roosevelt's Executive Order 9066 basically gave the government the authority to send all Americans of Japanese descent to concentration camps!"

"Internment camps." I corrected her, but couldn't really argue with her description.

"Smelly, unsanitary horse stables and dilapidated old barracks in the desert? The people could only bring what they could carry and, in some cases, had like seven days to sell all their businesses and non-mobile possessions."

"People like Aaron Smythe took advantage of the situation," I said.

"Apparently, you can get away with anything when your cousin is the chief of police," Sandy announced.

Didn't I wish? Was Aaron's cousin more amendable than Uncle G, or just on the take? I really needed to chat with Chelsea. She deserved a heads-up. Although nothing prosecutable had been found so far, embarrassment could result.

"The Barkview Bank appeared to be a fair custodian," Sandy admitted. "Though many of the internees lost their property to delinquent taxes."

Sure, if you had no revenue coming in... I'd expect nothing less than professionalism from the Barklays, who'd run the bank at that time.

"Smythe took advantage of the Japanese fear and desperation. The Barkview Industrial area he developed in the 1950s and 1960s had been a flower farm he bought for pennies on the dollar."

"Was that the Tanakas' farm?" I asked.

"No. It belonged to..." Computer keys clicked in the background. "Haruto Yamaguchi."

"Miyo's fiancé," I said. And Michael's great-uncle.

"Yes. Hiro Tanaka sold his flower farm to Haruto's father a week before Pearl Harbor."

My pulse jumped. The timing couldn't be a coincidence. "Like he knew it was going to happen."

"Everyone knew something was going to happen," Sandy insisted. "The Old Barkview Inn's guest list tells another totally crazy story too. There was something going on there."

She had my attention. "Like what?"

"I don't know yet. Known Nazi sympathizers populated the place from 1941 to 1944. Makes me wonder if Charles Smythe might have been a spy."

That I didn't expect. Had Paula considered it? It would explain a lot.

Sandy continued. "Jennifer is checking his wartime assignments. He worked with Paula as a radio interceptor with the Coast Guard before transferring to the Navy, which sent him to the Presidio. Naval Intelligence had a *Top Gun*–style spy school there. The man is a ghost after that, until he died on the USS *Indianapolis*. She found a brief reference to him in the Philippines in some recently unclassified documents."

If Charles was a spy, had he recruited Hiro? Had his interest in Miyo been because of her father? Why had he covered up Henry Jones's disappearance? Maybe there was more to Henry Jones's visit to Barkview than we knew.

Why did every new piece of information bring more questions than answers?

CHAPTER 16

Chad tailgated me right to my townhouse's driveway and blocked any exit with his car. I felt no real fear, but sent a quick text to Russ anyway. No sense taking any chances. Chad's financial need to find the Douglas Diamond's reward could make him unpredictable. I eyed him over my shoulder. Dressed in jeans and a Bark U sweatshirt, the youthful Leonardo DiCaprio look-alike stood in the driveway tapping his foot. Winston, my calf protector, thought so too. He growled at my feet, his neck hair lion's mane tall.

Chad raked his fingers through the longish top of his hip-styled hair. "Did you find the diamond?"

I had to appreciate his directness. "We found a cave with potential World War II significance." No sense hiding anything. Barkview would know soon enough.

"World War II?" Genuine confusion marked his frown. "Madame Orr said the diamond would be found on 'the eve of the east wind.' That's tonight."

That he'd made the connection didn't surprise me. For all

his spectacular Indiana Jones antics in the name of media on his blog, Chad did have a scientific mind.

"She also said, 'The golden sun will rise from the shifting sands.' Unless there's an earthquake." I shuddered, remembering the last round of quakes and aftershocks. I'd almost been buried alive in a secret cave. "The wind may not be anything more than an ambiguous reference."

A shark-bit raft couldn't have deflated any faster than his enthusiasm. Great. Not my normal glass-half-full kind of comment. I checked my Google watch. "I don't have a lot of time. Meet me on the back patio." No sense giving my nosey neighbors more fodder for gossip central, or up the Barkview odds favoring who would find the Douglas Diamond.

Chad's short nod and quick step toward the boardwalk indicated he understood my reasoning. Winston calmed right away. He nudged me toward the kitchen door. I didn't fight the herding thing. The dog meant well. Easier to go along and trip over him later.

I grabbed two water bottles from the refrigerator and joined Chad at my patio table. A warm breeze ruffled the umbrella, while the afternoon sky glowed a burnt orange that Crayola could only hope to duplicate.

"Sorry about the drama. I am no threat," Chad insisted. Though he didn't back down when Winston hugged my feet with his teeth bared. That no dog seemed to like Chad said something I didn't want to contemplate.

Ice shone in the man's once amiable blue eyes. "I just need to find the diamond."

I nodded. "I know about your mother's medical bills. I hear there's a trial..."

"She doesn't qualify." No disguising his bitterness.

Maybe there was no hope. "I don't know the specifics, but

maybe Aunt Char can help. At the very least she will make a call."

He stared at me for a full second before speaking. "I don't understand. Why would she do that for me?"

"Because we stand together in Barkview." The answer was simple. Maybe a new Bark U professor wasn't exactly family yet, but we did protect our own.

"I'd appreciate anything she can do." His head shake seemed pained as he returned to topic. "Do you think the cave was Jonathan Douglas's?"

I couldn't let his hope run unchecked. "I don't know. If it is, I'm not sure there's a diamond to be found any longer."

He ran his fingers through his hair. "You think whoever found the cave during World War II found the diamond?"

"Like I said, I don't know. We'll know more after the chief secures the area and we've had a chance to investigate."

He nodded. "Is there anything I can do to help?"

Had Chad orchestrated this meeting as an olive branch of sorts? Us working together made sense. "I could use your help looking up information at the National Archives."

"To investigate the World War II link?"

"Yes."

Chad's phone pinged. "Sure. I, uh, need to go." He sprinted to the exit gate. "I hope you're wrong about the diamond."

I did too.

CHAPTER 17

Brakes squealed outside my home moments after Chad departed. Just as well. Russ's ferocity rivaled that of a Marine battalion storming Iwo Jima. Winston darted beneath the coffee table without even a bark when Russ charged through the front door. Good thing I'd left it unlocked, or it would've been hanging from the hinges.

"Cat, are you...?" His instant threat assessment registered no danger before he crushed me into his embrace, his thudding heart the real indicator of his feelings.

I melted into his chest. "I'm sorry. I overreacted."

He held me tighter. "It's okay. You're safe. We'll talk on the way. We're late..."

Of course we were, but unlike me, Uncle G wouldn't leave Russ behind. I still picked up the pace, tripping over Winston as I put on water shoes and stuffed my wetsuit into a bag. Better to be prepared for diving.

Seven minutes later, I sat in Russ's Land Rover with Winston's belly spread across my lap, shedding long fawn-colored hairs on my black joggers. I really knew better. Khaki would've been the better wardrobe choice.

Russ rapid-fire sneezed. Winston ducked his head into my armpit. Like that was going to help. I opened my window, allowing the fur strands to escape. The fresh air helped a little. Russ's sniffles eased.

He navigated the afternoon beach traffic heading south on First Street as I filled him in on Sandy's Old Barkview Inn spy theory.

Russ shrugged. "The hotel would've been a good place to see and be seen. No surprise Will's grandfather would be in the know. A hotel manager interacts with everyone."

Which put the man in a precarious position. When did protecting your country trump respecting a guest's privacy? "He had to have known what was going on," I insisted.

"The Old Barkview Inn did thrive during a challenging period under his management," Russ pointed out.

True. I did tend to want my heroes to be faultless.

"What else is bothering you?" Russ asked.

"Henry Jones's dog tags. I know Uncle G claims the man survived the war, but why would Charles Smythe essentially erase his Barkview presence? Also, Haruto Yamaguchi's body was identified solely by a jade family ring since no other features were recognizable. And there is a body in the cave."

Two odd occurrences around the same time never worked for a coincidence nonbeliever like Russ either. "Let's see what we find in the cave."

He parallel parked behind Uncle G's police SUV in front of Lifeguard Tower One. Built more as a stationary beach changing room in the 1920s and then elevated to a lifeguard tower during the surf-crazy 1960s, the mint-green-and-white Victorian shack was nestled fifty yards from the tide pools and coastal cliffs due south of Bark Rock.

I shaded my eyes to study the iconic rock. Contrary to

popular opinion, I'd never thought the volcanic outcropping looked anything like a dog until now. Maybe it was the way the light cast shadows on the northeast-facing jagged peaks, but with a little imagination I could see pointed ears. The distant arc did sort of resemble a curled tail. Okay, now I was losing it.

I focused instead on the windswept beach. One of the four inflatables launched the moment Russ opened the passenger door. Winston took instant offense. He leaped off my lap, his full-speed Corgi hop-run combination kicking up globs of sand as he ran toward the shore. I laughed so hard I cried as the dog's on-a-dime pivot evaded Sandy's grab, toppling her into All-American Officer Richards, who caught her with tango flair at the cost of dropping a scuba tank inside the second hard-bottomed inflatable with a clankety-clank and an ear-piercing *psst* of escaping compressed air. No explosion, though, except the four-alarm-fire blush on Sandy's cheeks when Officer Richards set her on her feet.

The sand vibrated under Uncle G's intervention march. Winston, being a true self-preservationist, dashed toward the safety of the imposing Barkview Cliffs. In all fairness, the incident wasn't all his fault. Too many people loitered in too many directions for even a pint-sized genetic herder's tolerance. Listen to me making excuses for out-of-control dog behavior.

Naturally, Uncle G's scathing glare blamed me for everything. "Paula's granddaughter will be back in a day or so to take charge of him."

I wisely chose silence when he gestured for his deputy German Shepherds to pursue Winston. Good or bad? I wasn't sure. Nor about the odd little twinge somewhere near my heart. It was only a matter of time before I'd break a leg falling over that dog, but Winston made me laugh. Maybe it was his ever-present smile or his silly Corgi antics. No matter, the dog enjoyed life and made everyone around him appreciate it too.

Max and Maxine rounded up Winston with a simple divide-and-conquer strategy and herded the Corgi back to the pack. Winston huffed and splooted at Uncle G's feet, his tummy fur swiffering the damp sand. Ugh! I could already feel the grit on my quilt.

Uncle G directed his comment toward Russ. "We found the cave from your pictures and description. Chad Williams believes the May earthquakes shifted the rocks."

"Chad is here?" That had to have been the call he received at my home earlier.

"Yes. He is here to test the cave's structural integrity before we excavate," Uncle G added quickly, almost daring me to object.

I didn't. "Good. He should be here. His hunt for the Douglas Diamond makes him part of this legend too," I said.

Uncle G patted my arm. "I agree. He and the forensic anthropologist went out thirty minutes ago. We'll start clearing the entrance when her electronic measurements are completed. Be warned. We are dealing with a boulder choke."

"Large rocks or boulders obstructing the cave's entrance," Sandy explained. Although her cheeks had returned to peaches-and-cream wholesomeness, her eyes twinkled like Ceylon sapphires every time they turned toward Officer Richards. Hmmm.

Uncle G's nod didn't surprise me. Sandy really did know everything. "We'll need to break them up. We'll start with a rotary hammer drills and wedges. The structure appears to be too unstable even for a small blast."

On the positive side, we hadn't missed anything yet. Except the chance to be the first inside the cave, which—while disappointing to my reporter's mind, had been the right thing to do. I glanced at Russ checking our dive gear. Had to love the man's commitment to security.

"Is Victor Roma here?" I asked. Who had more reason to be on-site than the man offering the million-dollar recovery reward?

"No. I explained if we found the stone that there is a protocol we will follow." Uncle G's clipped words said way too much.

With real power hanging in the balance of the stone's recovery, I rather doubted patience had prevailed on Victor's part. The extra security surrounding this adventure suddenly made perfect sense.

"Let's find the diamond first," Russ suggested.

I agreed. We pulled on our wetsuits, leaving the tops unzipped and hanging from our waists. Preparation was one thing; sweating in the warm Santa Ana wind was quite another.

An odd peace settled over me as we launched into the choppy seas and motored toward Bark Rock. Was Madame Orr right that I wasn't destined to find the diamond? If so, then who was? And what were we going to find tonight? A World War II hideout?

I scratched Winston's ears, watching the sun hinge on the horizon—that moment when the day holds onto its last blast of light—illuminating Bark Rock in a red-orange halo. Sandy gasped when we turned the corner and Jonathan Douglas's phoenix symbol glowed like the X-marks-the-spot landmark it was meant to be to the left of the work crew.

We'd done it. Sandy and I shared a triumphant glance. Whatever else happened, we had deciphered hundred-year-old clues and found the long-elusive secret beach and smugglers hideout.

Russ high-fived us both. He tied our inflatable to another double-engine speedster and helped us out. On the rocky shore, huddled in front of the cave's sliver of an entrance, two men dressed in police windbreakers operated a hammer drill while Chad inserted wedges. Beside him, a small-statured woman in navy overalls with electric-blue-streaked hair pointed a laser at the next drill site. Despite their efforts, the opening hadn't increased by even an inch since we'd first seen it this morning. In fact, the drilling seemed to cause an earthquake-quiver beneath our feet. Dust even clouded overhead, promising a real storm.

Winston felt it too. His ears flat back, he backpedaled (which was weird to see his midget legs do) until he bumped his fluffy butt into the inflatable. The fearless explorer in full retreat? I tapped Russ's bicep. Even I heeded a dog's sixth-sense warning. Bark Rock's determination to keep its secrets might very well portend disaster.

Russ read the situation and quickly radioed the chief to halt the project. There had to be another way in. Sandy and I sat on the pontoon and watched. We were so close. I sensed victory.

Russ, Chad, and the forensic anthropologist, who'd introduced herself as Chris Gibbs, gathered around a map they'd laid across a rock, while the two policemen placed generator-operated spotlights. Although a head shorter than both men, Chris held her own. I admired her spirited insistence that they continue, even if she was wrong. "You're basing your decision on a dog's behavior?" No missing her exasperation.

How many times had I said that? On loan from San Diego PD and not Barkview broken-in, I got her skepticism.

"Come on, Chad. Why aren't you fighting this decision?" she demanded.

Chad's I'm-not-sticking-my-neck-out look didn't surprise me. Our supposedly fearless treasure hunter generally chose no decision as his decision. "We, uh, need more data before I can..."

I bit back a smile. Much as I wanted to get into the cave, I'd rather not sink the island to do so. Winston peeked over the dingy and barked his agreement, his happy Corgi smile back in place. I lifted him onto my lap. As the shadows lengthened, the phoenix symbol faded. So much for rebirth.

Sandy suddenly bounced in her seat, her eyes twinkling. "Jonathan Douglas proposed to Marie in March. It's September. That would change the sun's angle roughly 23.5 degrees to there." She pointed to the left of the current opening toward the original beach area we'd investigated before Winston had led us to the cave.

"The earthquake could've shifted..." I said.

"What if that fissure is just another way in? The entrance Jonathan used could've been directly beneath the symbol at low tide."

My pulse leaped. I couldn't help it. Her hypothesis made sense. The clues we'd assembled in search of the Douglas Diamond had indicated that the tide mattered. Too bad the boulder pile in the direct line offered little additional hope unless... "Grab the GPR," I said.

Sandy removed the case we'd used earlier and two head-lamps from the dinghy. The skip in her step influenced mine as we waded knee-deep into the cool Pacific. Winston remained on the beach, herding hermit crabs. Mission accomplished, he swam out, paddling in circles, his feet working like mini-oars while he sniffed under rocks and bit at phantom fish. At least I hoped there was nothing there.

I moved the ground-penetrating radar device across the rocks, mimicking Russ's methods as best I could from this morning, while Sandy manned the scanner. Had it only been twelve hours ago? It felt like a lifetime ago.

"Stop. Go back." Sandy's sharp command shocked me. I almost dropped the scanner.

"Is it...?" I was almost afraid to ask.

"Either the saltwater is affecting the readings, which is possible, or..."

"There's a tunnel?"

"An opening. Remember Bark Rock is like six feet shorter than it was in 1920."

"A collapsed cave." That thought tempered any runaway anticipation.

"We don't need to drive a semi into it," Sandy insisted. "I can't tell how big it is or if it's even connected, but..." She pointed to squiggles on the monitor.

I frowned. The opening looked to be about the size of the fissure the police crew had already tried to widen.

Sandy looked over my shoulder. "Winston?"

A dog might fit. "No way. I can't send the dog inside." In this town I'd be arrested for endangerment.

"I know. I wasn't suggesting. It's just..."

"We don't even know exactly where the opening is," I said.

"Winston does," Sandy pointed behind me.

I spun in time to see the dog's fluffy butt sticking out from beneath a rock shelf. I lunged after him too late. Like that last flash before sunset, he disappeared under the jutting edge.

Furballs! I pulled my arms through the wetsuit sleeves and crouched in the water, my headlight illuminating the craggy underside of the rock. Visions of chasing that adventurous Golden Doodle, G-Paw, through the speakeasy bolt-hole swamped me. Of course, this cave seemed even smaller. The half-hidden underwater part didn't help any either. On the positive side, this time no intermittent earthquakes threatened to bury me alive. I just needed to navigate through murky, knee-deep water, home to who knew what icky creatures. A lump stuck in my throat. The black unknown always sent my imagination into sci-fi land. As if I had a choice.

"Winston, come." Fear crept into my voice. I couldn't help it. I really, really hated cave diving. Was even thinking about going after him unsafe? "Winston. Come now."

No response over the ebb and flow of the water splashing against the rocks. How had I ended up with another explorer dog? That moment reaffirmed my last tunnel adventure's conclusion. Sit, stay, and come commands were necessities for saving lives, mainly mine.

A catch-me-if-you-can bark echoed inside the cave, making everything worse. This was no game. I peered into the darkness. My light illuminated about ten feet inside before a dark mass, likely a rock, blocked my view. Had Winston swum around it? How deep did the cave go? Did it lead to the current inaccessible room on the far side of the boulders? Did I dare leave Winston to find a way out on his own?

"I'll get him." Chad came up beside me, bare-chested and ready for action.

Knock me over. Mr.-Run-from-Danger offering assistance? Too bad I couldn't take it. "Your shoulders will never fit. Besides, considering your animal magnetism, that dog just might bite you for your trouble." I could kill Paula for dragging me into this mess.

"Get some light in here," I said. "I may need it to get out."

Before I came to my senses, I pointed my headlamp forward and entered the half-flooded cave no bigger than a submarine torpedo tube. The damp, moldy smell got to me right away. I wondered what toxins I was breathing in. This had to be some cosmic joke. Me, chase another dog into a dark, forbidding hole?

I sucked in my breath and swam forward, glad for the protection the wetsuit offered as I scooted through the cave, pushing off the slick walls. At first my knees brushed the rocky bottom, but the farther I swam, the deeper it got. I passed the first rock pile. A flash of fluffy white appeared ahead, then disappeared behind another dark object. I tried calling Winston to return, but I doubted he could hear me over the rhythmic slosh of the tide. I could hardly hear myself think.

Fear for the dog's safety compounded. How far could the short-legged Corgi swim? Winston had energy to spare in spurts. Sure, he had a flotation device on, but with no solid ground to rest, he could wear himself out and... I had to keep going. I glanced over my shoulder as the exit vanished into the darkness beyond my light beam.

My intuition twinged, and a crazy sense of déjà vu swamped me. Jonathan Douglas had been in this cave. I felt his fear—felt the walls closing in and rocks tumbling all around him as the ground shook its fury. OMG! The earthquake. He'd been buried alive in here!

I sucked in my breath and couldn't exhale. Something sizzled. My headlamp flickered. Once, twice. Pop! The light went dark, plunging me into total, black-void darkness. I tried to scream, but saltwater slapped into my mouth, choking me. I sputtered, floundering in the darkness.

Had the tunnel shifted beneath me? OMG! Was that an earthquake? My imagination went wild. The sound of the slapping waves pounded through my head at the same time the rock ceiling pulled at my hair. It seemed closer now, as if the water was rising, flooding the cave. The Douglas Diamond's legend came back to me. No doubt about it. When the tide came in, this cave would fill with seawater!

Had Madame Orr foreseen my demise moments before finding the Douglas Diamond? No. It couldn't be. She'd said my destiny was elsewhere. Anywhere else would be fine. Just not lost in a dark, underwater cave.

My heart rabbit-raced as sheer terror threatened. Only Russ's Zen-like voice repeating "just breathe" reined in my runaway panic. Keep moving, I told myself; he'd meet me half-way. He always did. We were better together. I knew it.

Winston's bark reverberated around me. Was he ahead of me or behind? I wasn't sure. I cut my hand on a sharp-edged rock but didn't dare stop as I felt my way along the wall to who knew where.

Sheer will kept me moving until something solid bumped my ribs. Another scream stuck in my throat as a slobbery tongue licked my face. "Winston." Wet fur brushing my face had never felt so good. Relief washed over me.

Saved by the stubborn, pint-sized Corgi? Who'd believe it? The dog swam under my arm and led me onward. I didn't fight him. Dogs had way better night vision than humans anyway. It felt like forever until a faint streak grew into a glow just ahead. Not any old glow, but high-intensity LED searchlights. Could it be the room beyond the rock fissure Russ and I had found?

I kicked toward it, towing Winston with me, swimming until my knees scraped sandy bottom and I crawled onto dry ground. Winston followed right behind. He puppy-shook and greeted me with another exuberant face lick. Ick! No escaping that bit of canine love, I guess. I scratched his head. We'd defi-nitely reached the World War II hideout. I recognized the radio Russ and I had seen earlier.

"Russ, I'm in here. I made it." I saw him through the rock crevice.

He didn't say a word. He didn't need to. The sheer relief glittering in his bright blue eyes said it all. He'd get me out of here if he had to knock down the wall himself. Which seemed possible, the way he shouted orders.

CHAPTER 18

Moments later, it seemed like high noon in the small chamber, if you could call the five foot crawl space anything but a cubby. Turned out our earlier sneak peek through the rocks had seen about all of it.

Good thing I'm not claustrophobic, I reminded myself, focusing instead on the signs of civilization scattered among the rubble. The area had definitely been struck by a catastrophic collapse, given the massive amount of volcanic debris and dust coating everything. Natural or manmade destruction? I'd let the experts figure that one out. With the tide rising, dry ground beneath my feet reassured me. It would be hours before the water level receded enough to exit the way I'd come in.

Except for my crazy vision of Jonathan Douglas while swimming through the cave, I found no 1920s period artifacts. In fact, this hideout resembled a 1940s California retreat. Even the canteen I salvaged from beneath a mangled metal chair fit the timeline. Although touted as noncorrosive, the Swiss-cheesed bottle was definitely not constructed from 1920s aluminum. Yes. I knew the difference. Recyclability had brought that product full circle. If this had been a Japanese relay station, why didn't I find any proof?

The real question was, had Jonathan taken refuge here? The 1940s resident could easily have helped himself to the treasure, but how had he found this cave? I glanced at the skeleton half hidden beneath rubble.

"Who are you?" I asked aloud. As if the skeleton could reply.

Could I have gotten this all wrong? The cipher we'd discovered earlier had not been in Japanese characters; it was alphanumeric. Russ's conclusion that the cave's destruction had been deliberate also came to mind. Had we stumbled upon a complex spy network? In Barkview?

I shuddered as I moved in for a closer look at the bones. If I could find even a clue...

"Don't touch anything!" Like a command from above, the order bounced off the rocks and echoed in my head.

I froze mid-step.

"Quick answers are tempting, but you could destroy identification evidence." I finally recognized Chris's voice.

"Can I tell you what I see?" Answers mattered for my peace of mind. I was the one stuck in here with the skeleton.

"Better yet, take pictures." An arm dangled a cell phone through the passage, shadowing the room. I reached for it. No luck. A good six inches separated our reach. Winston solved the problem. He brushed by my arm as he wiggled through the hole. I let him go. The dog could've abandoned me, but instead he'd returned to lead me to safety. I knew he wouldn't leave me now.

My faithful companion returned with a cell phone anchored beneath his collar. My phone, no doubt thanks to Sandy. Now I'd have a record of my own.

The moment I took control of the phone, Winston turned tail and wiggled his butt right back out the hole. He returned moments later, dragging a weighted soft backpack. Inside I discovered a water bottle, a chocolate power bar (I gobbled that right away), and a small blanket that I put to immediate use. Crazy as it sounded, my body warmed the moment I removed the damp neoprene wetsuit. This dog courier thing had possibilities.

No cell signal meant Winston would need to continue to run messages. Not that he minded. He sat at my feet, his usual Corgi smile in place and expressive ears following my every move. I filmed the space and focused in on the exposed skeletal parts. The torso had taken the direct hit and remained, for the most part, under debris, forcing me to concentrate on the skull.

Curiosity got me over the icky part quickly. Turns out that Halloween skeletons are all wrong. This skull's eyes appeared circular but lacked definition. And the heart-shaped nose just looked weird. Maybe the two gold teeth glittering in the video light could help with future identification, but even I knew that gold fillings had been used since the 1800s.

The moment I completed my task, Winston carried the phone to the outside world. He returned empty-pawed to wait with me. I thought about Chris's comment about disturbing evidence. If I stayed away from the body, I could continue explorations. I'm not sure what, but something pointed me toward the rock pile in the corner. Almost immediately, the Corgi tugged a pair of rubber soles out of the rocks. My pulse jumped. Something personal had to be a good sign. Encouraged, I cleared loose rocks until I discovered a rusted metal panel that appeared to be the remains of a storage cabinet.

I stretched my hunched back as best I could in the cramped space. Chris's excited shout for more close-up photos distracted me. I waited for Winston to return with the phone, took the requested pictures and sent him back through the tunnel.

I returned to the corner rock pile energized.

Winston joined me as I blew dust off a tarnished silver box about the size of an eight-by-ten picture frame and six inches tall. The scrollwork beneath the grime screamed antique—eighteenth century, judging from the aristocratic lady in the design. My heart raced. Marie Douglas had idolized Marie Antoinette. My hands shook as I searched the box for the clasp. I found it hidden in the inscription *Queen of My Heart* below the design.

OMG! The Douglas Diamond, I knew it. Had I found it?

My hand shook as I shone my flashlight directly on the box. I expected a brilliant yellow flash and an emotional power surge like I'd experienced holding the diamond's twin, the eighteen-carat Shepard Diamond. Knowing uniting the two stones could very well change the world order made it even better. I sucked in my breath, hardly daring to breathe as I lifted the lid....

Nothing! I exhaled in a rush. No! The box was empty. I tipped it over just to be sure. The tattered remains of moldy velvet fluttered to the ground. I glanced at the skeleton. If that was Jonathan Douglas, the 1940s resident had likely taken the stone. If not, Jonathan could've taken the necklace with him when he'd run from this chamber. Why did that scenario feel wrong? Because the box would mean as much as the necklace to Marie. The realization hit me squarely. Someone else had the Douglas Diamond, and they'd had it for a long time.

I rushed back to the opening. "Chris, can you tell if the skeleton is Asian or Caucasian?"

"I can't be certain without placing the jawbone on a flat surface."

Ugh! If I wanted answers now, I'd have to touch it. I hesitated about a second and then cleared the flattest rock I could find and retrieved the skull. I ignored the shiver. "What am I looking for?"

"European mandibles, I mean jawbones, tend to undulate, or rise and fall along the lower jaw border. The gonia–that's the area beneath your ears where the jawbone turns upward— are more likely to have a flatter edge in Europeans."

I set the skull on the rock. No rises or light shining under it. It seemed to lay perfectly on the surface. "It doesn't look anything like that."

Hard to miss the catch in her voice. She had an idea. The scientist in her just needed confirmation. "Send me a video."

I did—hopefully, the best I'd ever done—and hurried my Corgi courier through the tunnel. Minutes ticked by in slow motion. I wanted to pace, but the walls just closed in on me further. I chewed my lip until I heard Chris's triumphant aha!

I jumped, banging my head on the low ceiling. Patience had never been my best attribute. I had to ask. "What?"

"I'll need to do more testing, but my best guess is the skull is Asian."

Deep down, I'd known it all along. I just hadn't wanted to believe a traitor lurked in Barkview. The question loomed, was the body in Haruto Yamaguchi's grave his? Or Hiro Tanaka's? What part did Miyo play?

Which brought us full circle. Until I found the Barkview traitor who'd supplied information to the Japanese, I'd never know what had happened to the Douglas Diamond.

CHAPTER 19

Exiting the cave turned out to be far less stressful than getting in. No, Russ did not blow the walls down in a grand rescue, though I know he would have if given the chance. Patience prevailed, and I waited out the tide change thanks to a little help from my FedEx dog, who delivered my every need on command. We'll get into the obedience thing later. I ended up swimming out of the cave ten or so hours later with the help of a reliable high-powered dive light. Russ met me halfway. His salty kiss tasted wonderful.

I managed to get a couple of hours of catnap before waking up energized and ready for answers. My first stop was to see Chelsea Smythe.

Hana, whom I'd met at the dojo, greeted me when I strolled into Adam Smythe's congressional campaign office, located in a Victorian storefront mid-block on Fourth, between Sycamore and Oak Streets. Apparently in his element, Adam inspired a gathering of supporters. The man had charisma, I'd give him that.

"Good morning, Miss Wright. Chelsea will meet you in the conference room. Please follow me." Dressed in a conservative pencil skirt with a matching navy jacket sporting a patriotic campaign button, her hair in a neat bun, Hana looked every inch a political strategist as she directed me away from the crowd. No wonder Chelsea had hired her. "Is it true you found the Douglas Diamond?"

No surprise that the Barkview rumor mill had gotten that one wrong. Everyone wanted a happy ending. Winston's response surprised me. The dog gave Hana a long once-over, then nudged my ankles. I grabbed a wall for balance. Ugh! I really hated it when he diverted me. "I'm afraid not. We found a cave. The proper authorities are excavating now."

Her wry smile didn't exactly call my bluff. "You have quite the story to report."

"Not sure that I do." Winston prodded me again. This time more vigorously. What didn't he like about this place?

"I don't understand. You report what you see?" Hana gestured for me to precede her into the conference room.

No way was Winston allowing that. He blocked the doorway. I stuck my head inside. No threat under the twelve-seat cherrywood table or near the big-screen TV. Was this about Adam Smythe?

I stepped carefully over the trip-hazard dog, glad I'd chosen to wear bend-with-you light-colored slacks and a white blouse. I sat in a high-backed swivel chair facing the door. Winston plopped on my feet, crushing my toes. "There are some stories that are not mine to tell."

"And here you are hours after escaping from a cave to meet with Chelsea. Perhaps it's her story?" Those perceptive blue eyes saw far more than I'd intended.

No sense denying a thing. "That would be up to her."

Hana's *hmm* seemed telling.

"What will be up to me?" Chelsea Smythe breezed through the doorway with her late mother's champion Blenheim King Charles Cavalier, Lady Mag, matching her stride. I silenced Winston's growl with a nudge.

"Whether you pour me a Woofing Best caramel cappuccino, or we go out for one." I meant it too. "I haven't had my second cup yet."

"You're scaring me," Chelsea admitted with a smile.

"I'll go," Hana volunteered. "Two extra-large caffeine fixes coming up."

She reminded me of Sandy, the way she scurried out the door. "A tea drinker?"

"You know it." Chelsea took the strategic center-of-the-table seat. Dressed in tailored navy slacks and a white blouse beneath a coordinating jacket, she reminded me so much of her late mother I blinked. Except for her hair. Chelsea had modernized her look from a neat chignon to a feathered bob that skimmed her collar. "What's so critical you haven't had your second cup of coffee yet?"

I really wished I had good news. Despite the adversarial mayoral campaign between her father and my aunt, we'd managed to forge a working relationship during the Shepard Diamond investigation. We were still a long way from besties. "I have credible information implicating Aaron Smythe in treason."

My bluntness worked. Her gasp sounded like a something-stuck-in-your-throat croak. "Let me understand. You have information which at this point must be hearsay, alleging that over eighty years ago a long-dead relative may have committed a crime?"

Phrased that way, it sounded ridiculous. "This is Barkview." Which really said it all.

She sank into the swivel chair. Like it or not, she got it. Legalese meant nothing in the court of public opinion. And Barkview demanded a higher standard for their heroes.

"And you are here because...?" she asked cautiously.

"As a courtesy for you to get ahead of it. The authorities will be in the cave later today. I don't know exactly what they'll find, but you know what the chief's like when he gets a bone. What I have is damning." I let the words sink in.

"What do you want?" Her seasoned tone spoke of too much experience. How many of her father's questionable past political favors had she already dealt with?

"The truth."

Chelsea eyed me. "You're questioning Paula's information?"

"Yes." I didn't ask how she knew I had it. Barkview's gossips had done well.

"It's common knowledge that my great-uncle CJ Smythe legitimized all of the Smythes' holdings," she admitted.

Nothing unknown there. "Do you have records dating back to the 1940s?"

"I don't know. My father and uncle have the key."

My turn to frown. "What is the key?" But I knew. The Barkview Bank's wall of legacy safe deposit boxes came to mind.

"I see you know. You received Paula's. Why did you get it? It was her granddaughter's right," Chelsea said.

"Paula wanted answers she knew I would pursue."

"In the name of the truth, with no thought for the consequences."

I got her bitterness. "I think you know me better than that."

"You're right. That was unfair. I wonder at what point those secrets become too much even for you."

Or too dangerous. But that was another story.

"Sometimes I wonder if ignorance isn't bliss," Chelsea mused.

"Aunt Char says the same thing," I replied.

"Interesting comment from the woman who inherited the Barklays' key."

No kidding. I hadn't thought about that. No doubt Aunt Char knew far more than I thought. That meant one day I would get it. Oddly, my curiosity just froze. Chelsea said it best. How many secrets were enough?

"I can't promise anything, but what information specifically are you looking for?" Chelsea asked.

"We believe a spy passed critical information about landing site weaknesses to the Japanese fleet from 1941 to 1942."

Chelsea steepled her hands. "Anyone involved in the construction could've provided it."

"The traitor operated over a ten-month period, requiring land-based supplies."

Chelsea suddenly sat upright. "Delivered by courier dogs."

I recognized her light-went-on expression. She definitely knew something. No need to prompt her; she explained right away.

"It was a bedtime story my dad told me years ago about a dog that helped end a war."

My turn for surprise. Generational stories, like legends, tended to be based in some truth. Or covered a lie.

Hana returned with our coffee, stalling Chelsea's big reveal. The interruption helped. We both needed time to absorb what we'd shared. Chelsea thanked Hana and excused her, but Hana clearly wanted to stay. She focused her beseeching look on me.

I shrugged. This wasn't my story to tell.

With no help forthcoming, Hana closed the door behind her. I took a long satisfying swallow of my caramel cappuccino and settled into my chair.

Chelsea glanced skyward, clearly remembering. "The story was about a Cavalier named Ginny. Ginny Hall, the famous spy, I'd guess. The princess's castle was under attack, and the dog swam from the palace to a secret island and delivered messages that tricked the enemy. The dog saved the kingdom. And everyone lived happily ever after."

"A Cavalier?" I glanced at the Blenheim Cavalier preening at Chelsea's feet. My aunt's Cavalier wouldn't even get her feet wet.

"I told you it was fantasy." Chelsea still stroked Lady Mag's head.

"Maybe partial truth," I suggested.

Chelsea stood. This meeting was over. "I'll see what I can find. How long do we have before this will get out?"

"You won't make it to election day."

She nodded.

"I'll report the news. Make it your story, Chelsea," I said.

Chelsea's smile widened. No doubt any information to be found would be shared. "I appreciate that."

I paused in the doorway, in earshot of every curious somebody. "It should be you on the ballot, Chelsea. You have what it takes to be a fair and capable legislator."

Chelsea's blush indicated she'd at least thought about it. "I like being behind the scenes."

That sounded too familiar. "The funny thing about walking one step behind someone else is at some point you have something to say."

With that truism resonating, at least in me, I left Smythe

campaign headquarters, pondering just how far Adam Smythe would go to get elected.

Next stop, the Old Barkview Inn. I now knew the right question to ask Will.

CHAPTER 20

I tried to ignore KDOG studio as I drove toward the Old Barkview Inn. Visions of two days of unanswered questions and issues piled on my desk messed with my focus until I made a right on Oak Street. Frankly, finding answers loomed larger than any administrative duty. Sure, the puzzle looked more like a blurred blob for now, but clarity came in pieces. I had a good idea of what had happened to Paula. The Douglas Diamond remained the big unknown. Someone had kept its location a secret for a long time. Maybe too long for the truth to ever come out.

With that depressing thought, I turned right on First Street and drove under the Victorian portico into the Old Barkview Inn's valet parking lane. The normally comforting smell of beeswax and fine wood upped my anxiety as I hurried through the grand foyer en route to the Centurion Otis 61 elevator and pressed the call button.

Winston paced as we waited for the majestic machine's descent. No surprise registered in Will's greeting as he slid open the ornate gate. He'd known I'd be coming back. "Welcome, Miss Wright, Master Winston. What can I do for you?" That he didn't scratch Winston's ears said as much as the visible hunch in his shoulders.

I wouldn't want to have this conversation either. No sense prolonging the inevitable. Post-its and pen ready (shockingly, I had a pen this time), I asked, "The right questions are, who cared for the Shiba Inus, and where were they housed?"

His deflated expression confirmed my suspicions. His grandfather had been the traitor. "When did you know?" I asked. Will idolized the man who had saved the Old Barkview Inn.

"When Paula asked about Henry Jones and I found the records in my box."

"You have a safe deposit box too?"

Will's pressed-lip nod was confirmation.

Of course, the Oldemans had a box. They were one of Barkview's founding families. "Where did your grandfather house the dogs?"

"In the Conti basement. He stored most of the Old Barkview Inn's treasures there during the war." He quickly clarified. "The Inn was a different place in 1942. Invasion fears and a steady stream of military personnel turned the hotel into a boarding house."

"The Conti basement?" First time I'd heard that beach level parking garage that housed the antique cars called that. "When was it constructed? It doesn't exist on any drawings."

"The basement isn't owned by the Old Barkview Inn."

That made no sense. It was directly beneath the hotel.

"Giuseppe Conti had it built in the 1930s as a separate entity."

"Aaron Smythe's company built it?" It wasn't really a question. The Smythes built everything at the time.

Will nodded. So Aaron Smythe had known about the secret

space too. No doubt he'd used it for his own nefarious purposes. "Why?"

"My grandfather does not say, but I'm sure you can guess why a Chicago gangster who bought a West Coast hotel would build secret rooms," Will said.

I suppose I could. Just thinking about how many bad guys had taken refuge in our idyllic seaside paradise about made me gag. Talk about a secret better left unsaid.

Fortunately, it didn't matter to this investigation. "Your grandfather aided and abetted a spy."

"So it appears."

"Why?" I really needed to know.

"My guess would be to buy back the hotel his father had lost during the Depression." Will's admission clearly tore at him.

"Many businesses went bankrupt during that time..."

"Pride." Will's single-word reply pretty much said it all.

"He was paid that well?"

Will ran his fingers through his hair. "My grandfather's notes reference a big payoff coming."

My heart thumped. "I take it he never received it."

"No. In October 1942, all communication ended."

That fit with the earthquake timeline. "What happened to the dogs?"

"One was turned over to the Coast Guard, the other to the Navy."

Now, the big question. "Do you have the Douglas Diamond?"

"What? N-no!" His shock couldn't be feigned.

I believed him. The Japanese spy hadn't paid off his supplier. Or had he? "Where did your grandfather get the information to send to the spy?"

Will frowned. Sharing this information hurt. "I'd intended to take this information to my grave."

"Until the next generation gets"—I made the quote symbol with both forefingers—"'the box.' Your nephew, right?"

Will shook his head. "The kid has no respect for the past."

How many adults said that about the youth of America? "He's only a teenager." If I remembered correctly. "He has plenty of time to improve with your help."

Will's pained exhale said otherwise. "I'm not the guy the kid wants to chill with." Hipster slang from the quintessential Victorian hurt my ears.

"The kid is a gamer." That explained nothing. "No. You will be the keeper of the Oldemans' secrets, Miss Wright."

"Me!" Should I be honored or terrified? Paula's secrets had about killed me just yesterday.

"You will do the right thing."

I about choked on the sudden lump in my throat. Will made it sound like a solemn vow. Before I could object, Will continued, "Enough of that. I do not intend to give this duty to you anytime soon. My grandfather lived to a hundred and six."

Honestly, I didn't want to know how many more years that represented for Will. Better to focus on the problem at hand. "Did your grandfather get the information from Charles Smythe?" It made too much sense.

Will hung his head. "Paula didn't want to believe it until she checked the Smythes' government contract files. She pieced together that Charles had access to them at the time of the transmissions."

If Charles had been a spy as Jennifer thought, I wondered exactly what information had been transmitted.

"Paula swore Miyo was involved," Will announced.

"Miyo? How?" According to Paula, Charles had protected the woman, but... "Miyo disappeared in December 1941."

"I agreed with you until Paula told me that Charles took possession of Miyo's Shiba Inu when the dog was transferred to the Navy. The dog vanished right after that."

Odd, but... "Paula thought Charles knew where Miyo was?"

"I don't know if it was wifely intuition or jealousy. She never found proof."

"Paula wants me to prove it now," I told him.

"I know. I told her she might be better served not shaking this tree," Will said. "The curious part is that Charles shipped out in March 1942. Grandfather continued activities until October. If Charles had been the informer, who provided the information from March until October?"

A good point. "Who was the Japanese spy?"

"My grandfather refers to him only as H."

Haruto Yamaguchi or Hiro Tanaka?

"Grandfather's notes also said that the cipher was plain Katakana. I don't know how he knew that or became proficient at it."

"Katakana is character-based. The cipher I saw was alphanumeric."

Will removed a folded paper from his breast pocket. "I knew you'd be coming for this." Will handed me two sheets of paper, both yellowed with age. "That's how the information came from the Smythe contact."

One showed the faded letters and numbers in the exact jumble of nothing like the note I'd found in the cylinder. The other bore Japanese characters. I quickly fumbled with my phone and took pictures. Best to get these to Sandy and Jennifer to expedite the translation.

"Your grandfather served in World War I, right?" I asked.

"Yes. First Expeditionary Forces in Toul, France."

Toul, France. Familiarity tugged at my memory. "What did he do during World War I?"

151

"I don't know. He never spoke about it. I remember sneaking up on him as a kid and him saying, *Chut, j'ecoute.*"

Will continued, "It translates to 'Shh, I'm listening.'"

"Listening to what?"

"I don't remember any longer. I found a black metal insignia in the family box. It had two crossed flags over a torch."

My intuition came alive. I Googled the description. "Signal Corps. Radio intercept."

Our eyes met. "He was a codebreaker." Just like Hiro Tanaka. This was no coincidence. Nor that the man presided over a hotbed of spies and intelligence gathering. The first William Oldeman had not been a traitor. He'd been working with Charles Smythe. I'd bet my Woofing Best Coffee on it.

Then who was the traitor? And where was the Douglas Diamond?

CHAPTER 21

No avoiding my KDOG studio office after leaving the Old Barkview Inn. My *Inbox Full* alert on my phone guilted me into suspending Paula's quest, at least until I found my desktop. I did detour to pick up lunch for Sandy and me. I always thought better on a full stomach.

Sandy met me at my office door. I almost missed her mischievous grin as I focused on the steaming caramel cappuccino she handed to me. I didn't know how she did it, but she neatly stepped over Winston as she relieved me of the lunch bag.

"Hana, from Adam Smythe's campaign, came by to see you. She said she has information you need to hear. She said she'd be back in an hour."

"She didn't want to talk to you?" Most people preferred Sandy's girl-next-door style to my directness.

"She insisted that she speak with you."

I could guess what an idealistic staffer on the Smythe campaign wanted to talk about. Needless to say, in a day of revelations, this one hardly registered. Sandy sat in my not-socomfy office chair with her laptop on her lap and listened as I explained what I'd learned from Will.

"You think Will's grandfather was a spy too?" Sandy asked.

"Maybe. I suspect he was a World War I codebreaker." I showed her the *Chut, j'ecoute* mantra on the Google search page techno-idiot me found. Maybe there was hope for me. "He had the know-how."

Sandy chewed her lip. "Jennifer and I are close to breaking the cipher. It's kind of like a hangman game now. We know enough letters to guess the rest. We think the note you found is a shopping list."

That was disappointing. "And Will's note?"

"The code in that note seems to be a complicated mix of letters and numbers, but no real words."

"Are there odd symbols?" I reached for Paula's notebook in my bag.

She nodded.

"I bet they're coordinates. You have degrees, seconds, and minutes." I handed her the leather book.

Sandy's back straightened. "This could be it." She tapped info into her phone. "Paula's coordinates show San Diego Harbor's 1940 beach defenses."

"And weaknesses. Very helpful for a Japanese invasion," I remarked.

Sandy popped to her feet. "I'll get this to Jennifer. She sent the Katakana to a friend who knows about it. If this matches..."

Had to love friends with skills. "It would potentially implicate Aaron Smythe." I told Sandy about Chelsea's dog courier story.

"You think Charles Smythe was feeding flawed information to the Japanese?" Sandy asked.

"Maybe. Anything on Henry Jones yet?"

"It's a common name. I'm searching, but not knowing

where he went after leaving the Navy makes the search..." She sighed. "It will take time."

"You'll find him, Sandy." I smiled. "If anyone can, you will do it. I have faith."

Sandy's smile lit up the room. "What if the Barkview Henry Jones was a spy too? This town seemed to have a lot."

Russ would say no way, but I wasn't so sure. "What if they were all working together?" Somehow that thought made some sense.

"On the bright side, the suspect list is shrinking." The eternal optimist, I appreciated Sandy's humorous interjections as she scooted out the door.

Alone with only Winston's snores to distract me, I glared at the to-do mountain on my desktop. If I burned the pile, would anyone even notice?

No answers forthcoming, I focused on decluttering. I'm not certain how long KDOG business monopolized my attention before Winston growled. That trouble-is-here sound made me reach for the stun gun in my top drawer until I saw Hana frozen in the Corgi-blocked doorway. Not that I blamed her for pausing. Although short, the dog had a big bite.

"Winston, sit." I swear he rolled his eyes and barked again. The dog's lack of obedience really needed immediate attention. "I apologize." I walked around my desk and nudged Winston aside to greet her with a handshake. Although her physical response indicated strong and capable personality traits, I sensed a vulnerability I'd not seen in our previous meetings.

"I can offer you coffee or water," I said.

"I'm fine, thank you. I saw the Pulitzers in the lobby. The *Bark View* has quite a past."

Severe politeness never boded well, nor did her grip on the canvas messenger bag she clutched across her chest as if her life depended on it. Anticipation hummed through me. What-ever she had to say had to be good. If I could get her to talk.

"Yes. Filling my aunt's shoes is a challenge." Not literally. Her size eleven pumps looked clownish on me.

"I'm confident you handle it just fine," Hana said.

Her sincerity touched me.

"Thank you for encouraging Chelsea to run for office. She needed to hear it from you," Hana said.

"I rather doubt anything I say matters much."

"No. She admires you." True or not, Hana believed it.

Was that why she'd come to see me? "I spoke the truth."

"Which is why I'm here." She twirled a pendant on a gold chain around her neck.

I reached for my coffee to give her a minute to compose herself. "I'll listen, but I must warn you that Adam Smythe is no model citizen."

Confusion marred her peaches and cream complexion. "I'm here about Charles Smythe."

"Charles?" I about spewed the sip of hot liquid I'd just taken. Hana's visit to Barkview was not just about getting experience in campaigning. I felt it.

Her voice jumped an octave higher. "He was my great-great-grandfather."

Talk about a bomb of a secret! My heart rate spiked as the truth hit me like a brick. Her Eurasian looks made perfect sense. "You're Miyo's great-great-granddaughter too."

Hana's nod confirmed so many things. "I came to Barkview to meet my Smythe relatives."

"And perhaps claim your heritage," I suggested. How many times did a long-lost child show up to claim part of the inheritance?

"No! Greatpa Charles said I looked like his mother. I was named for her."

156

Impossible! Charles Smythe died in 1945. "You spoke to him?"

"Every day until he died five years ago. He was ninety-nine." She blinked away a tear and stroked the gold pendant around her neck.

The shape held my gaze. It was a medallion. Charles's missing Saint Christopher pendant? "Are you telling me Charles Smythe survived World War II?" It wasn't possible. Where had he been for almost eighty years?

She nodded. "He asked me to come here. He said all the people he could hurt were long gone. He said he owed his wife the answers she sought."

"By abandoning her and making her a bigamist?" Paula would've loved that.

"He and Greatma Miyo never married. They lived as man and wife, though."

"He still abandoned his wife and son." Charles's note to CJ suddenly made perfect sense. Forgive his selfishness.

Hana removed tattered books from her bag. "I do not seek forgiveness, but to offer truth. I'd hoped you of all people would understand." She presented the books with both hands, a traditional Japanese gesture of trust. "Perhaps no one will. The answers you are looking for are in Miyo's words." She rose. "It's quite remarkable."

The books had vertical kanji text and an intricate, albeit faded, watercolor floral border on aged paper. The volumes felt warm to my touch.

Hana's fidget alerted me. There was more. I yoga-breathed. "I'm afraid to ask."

"I, uh, saw Paula the night she died."

I gasped. I couldn't help myself. Winston growled. I swear he flipped me an I-told-you-so look. Had he been trying to tell me that since meeting Hana?

157

Hana's voice shook. "I didn't kill her. She was yelling at me when that dog chased me out." Her finger shook as she pointed at Winston.

Winston's snarl confirmed his part. I stilled the pounding in my ears.

Hana continued. "Paula guessed everything right away. She called me the ghost of mothers-in-law past. It was surreal."

More like creepy. And so like Paula.

"I tried to deliver the books. She threw them back at me and called my greatma horrible things. Then got quiet and just said, 'I should've known.'"

"Should've known what?" I asked. But I knew too. Paula had gotten her answers. Closure was a good thing. Right?

"I don't know. She ordered the dog to get me out."

Winston's bared teeth seemed to concur. I stilled him with a sit command. He licked his paw, his eyes on us both.

"Do you think Sensei Michael knows anything? His grandfather died when he was a child."

Michael might not have all the answers, but he knew something. I'd bet another bag of Woofing Best Coffee that Michael had a box like the rest of our Barkview families. Question was, what secrets had his ancestors left him to deal with?

I assured Hana I would read the books. I started the moment she left. The three diaries spanned ten years and were works of art worthy of preservation. Written on newsprint paper, they had some spotting and staining around the edges, but that was all. The simple string bindings had detached. The plain kraft covers were decorated with detailed watercolor flowers, one with red California poppies and the other two with Hawaiian orchids. Miyo's narrative engaged me right away. So much so, I swear I heard a Japanese koto playing in the background. I was there in 1941.

December 7, 1941: What we have feared has happened. We are at war with Japan. The Navy needs Father in Hawaii. I will miss Charles. Father says it is our duty to protect our home. My heart breaks but I must return my beautiful Shiba Inu to Haruto. I cannot marry him feeling as I do.

December 26, 1941: We live on an old pineapple plantation northwest of Pearl Harbor.

The house is old. Mother sweeps the red dust all day. It never ends. It is lonely here without Charles. I cannot write to him. No one can know we are here. There is much anger here post Pearl Harbor. We live under martial law with curfews and military patrols on every corner. Fears the Japanese will invade are high. A car picks up father daily. He cannot tell us what he is doing. I know it is important. Father brings me word puzzles in Katakana. They keep my mind busy since I cannot go to school. I am quite good at them.

February 19, 1942: The news says President Roosevelt ordered all people of Japanese ancestry to internment camps. I am an American. I left Japan as a child. My Issei friends were born in America. They have never been to Japan. We are not criminals.

159

February 29, 1942: I have dishonored my family. I should feel shame. I do not. I love him. Mother is enraged. She forbids me to tell father or Charles. She will raise my child as her own. I do not know how I will feel.

April 10, 1942: I discovered a pattern in the word game father brought me. It is not Katakana, but something different. I think it is in code. The words did not make sense, but father understood. He wouldn't explain, so I unpacked a box of his old Navy books. The words make sense now. Father is breaking the Japanese naval code. I am helping. We are both loyal Americans.

I knew it. I took a deep breath. This story read better than a Hollywood blockbuster. History gave Station HYPO credit for breaking the JN-25 code and winning the Battle of Midway, but had that been the whole truth? Had an immigrant Japanese father and his math whiz daughter really done it? Mom would rally behind this truth. The world needed to know.

Sandy's blonde head peeked into my office. "Jennifer's friend translated the katakana code. The battery coordinates were fake."

"The coordinates would've put any attack force in the direct line of fire," I said.

"Yes. Charles was feeding false information to the Japanese. How did you know?" Sandy asked.

I raised Miyo's books and motioned for her to sit as I continued to read aloud. My eyes misted when Hiro Tanaka gave his life protecting his adopted country in 1944 and the family was released from military protection. Miyo's code work and translation skills paid the bills for housing and food.

Months went by without an entry, until she saw Charles Smythe by chance at Pearl Harbor.

August 2, 1944: Charles is a spy. He cannot hide the truth from me. Mother forbids me from telling him about his son, Akira. I say he has a right to know. I would have told him anyway until he showed me a picture of his son, CJ. He is so proud. I understand now, the boy is a true Smythe. Mother was right that Akira is father's legacy.

August 10, 1944: Charles left for the Philippines. He thinks I do not know. I coded his message. I wonder if I will see him again.

April 5, 1945: Charles is injured. He is at the naval hospital. He saw Akira and me. He knew the moment he saw him. I cried in happiness. We fell in love all over again.

May 8, 1945: We celebrated V-E Day today. The end must be near, but every day I see a new headstone and every bed is filled with injured soldiers, some so young. This war will change much. I spend more time with the Japanese American soldiers. They need to feel appreciated too.

June 1, 1945: Charles leaves for weeks at a time, but I know he will return. He cares for Akira, me, and mother. He found us a home with an ocean breeze. When he showed up with my Shiba Inu, I knew Haruto was dead. Charles said he'd died in an earthquake, sending false information to the Japanese fleet.

"Haruto was a hero?" It did not sound like him.

Charles's smile told me without saying. Haruto had been a Japanese spy. Loving Charles and refusing to marry Haruto saved me from being a Yamaguchi and feeling that family's shame.

June 4, 1945: Charles came to say goodbye. I knew he'd been ordered stateside on a Pan Am Clipper. Twenty-one hours in an airplane frightened me. Something big was happening. I felt the energy at Station HYPO. He promised to take care of me and Akira. I reminded him he had a family and as long as he lives his loyalty must be to the Smythes. I recognized the pain in his eyes. Akira's is the same. Charles knows I am right.

I will care for my family. I must. My heart broke as he walked away. There was no other way for us.

July 30, 1945: Charles died when the USS Indianapolis sank. I uncoded the first message.

I worked all day while my heart broke.

October 4, 1945: A man limped to my door. I had to be dreaming. He looked like Charles, but that was impossible. He'd died when the Indianapolis went down. I'd cried over the casualties. It was Charles. He'd been injured in the USS Indianapolis blast and was found unconscious wearing his friend's dog tags. He claimed it was a case of mistaken identity, but I knew better. I hugged him tight. His arms around me felt so right. I never wanted it to end.

"I'm here if you'll have me. No family. No past. Just a strong back and the commitment to care for you and yours," he told me.

I pulled away. "Your wife?"

"Is a Smythe. She will be cared for, and my son, CJ, will take his rightful place."

"I will not be your responsibility."

"Will you be my love?"

I knew then that Charles Smythe had orchestrated it all. Partially from his deep sense of responsibility, but mostly for love.

"So it was a love story." Sandy wiped a tear from her dreamy eyes. "He gave up everything for her."

"To take care of the family only he could." I had to correct her. It had always been about family. That was what Charles had wanted Paula to know. She would've understood—not forgiven, but accepted it. It was the same deep commitment I'd sensed in Russ–the kind that lasts a lifetime.

"Who was Henry Jones?" Sandy asked.

"Someone Charles worked with who got caught up in the Japanese spy conspiracy. And an easy identity for Charles to claim, considering the circumstances."

"How did Charles know he was dead?" Sandy asked.

I shrugged. "I guess when the body washed up in Barkview and Henry Jones never showed up, Charles knew something had happened to him. Why else would he erase the man's existence in Barkview?"

"We will never know for sure, will we?" Sandy asked.

Probably not. I shook my head. I got why Charles had done it. I also knew who killed Paula and why. The question was, could I prove it?

CHAPTER 22

I parked in front of the dojo. As expected, Michael sat cross-legged deep in meditation on the mat inside. A true creature of habit, he practiced his Zen-like calm daily before afterschool activities started.

Russ and Uncle G parked a few cars behind. I'd tried to reason with them. Michael would never hurt me, but they'd both insisted on being on watch anyway. I wore a bug too. Not the crawly kind, just a microphone hidden in my correctly tied purple belt that Russ wouldn't allow me to enter Kanine Karate without.

I stumbled over Winston as I entered. I was ready this time and caught the handle before sprawling. I was definitely getting used to the Corgi's quirks. I readjusted my gi and the leather cross-body bag I'd carried Miyo's diaries in under Michael's one-eyed glance. I'd planned it that way. It made my announcement all the more impactful.

"The chief is coming with a court order to exhume Haruto's body for DNA testing," I said.

Michael's reflective breathing did not waver. Had I imagined an ever-so-slight crease in his brow? "You found him." No question in his tone. Just resolve.

"How did Haruto find the cave?" I asked.

"By chance. His fishing boat ran out of fuel. He took refuge on Bark Rock. His Shiba Inu found the tunnel."

I relaxed. "Why did your grandfather dynamite the cave's entrance?"

"To bury the truth," he admitted. "The earthquake closed off access to the cavern, but he feared another could reopen it."

"It lasted eighty years." Michael's nod agreed. My theory had been right on so far.

"Henry Jones's family deserves closure too. What happened?" But I knew.

"According to my grandfather, Henry Jones followed the Shiba Inu couriers to the cave. Haruto killed him in self-defense."

While committing treason, but that wasn't important now. "Why did Haruto sell US government secrets?"

"There was much anger back then. The internment order..."

"He started before the order," I had to add. "October 1941, to be exact."

"Discrimination and retaliation against the Japanese started as far back as 1939."

He didn't need to say that Haruto had been harassed. It all added up.

"Miyo pushed him too far."

"Miyo?" I asked. What part did she play?

"She refused to marry him."

"Miyo refused to marry him because she was pregnant with Charles Smythe's child." No shock. Not even a blink. He'd known. "Paula told you the night she died."

In a single graceful motion, Michael stood, towering over

me. I'd forgotten just how intimidating he could be. Show no weakness, I reminded myself, and held my ground.

"You know about Miyo too." It wasn't a question. "Paula wouldn't tell me how she'd discovered it."

I removed Miyo's diaries from the pouch. Michael's gaze locked on the simple kanji text cover. "It was the last missing piece. Paula figured it all out when she met Hana."

Michael's exhale seemed strained. A break in his calm?

"Paula threatened to tell all on your show. My son is a three-star Navy admiral. If this information became public, it would have ended his career," Michael said.

"Not for something a relative did eighty years ago," I insisted.

"You don't understand."

But I did. I wondered if Michael did. The values of one generation didn't always matter as much to the next. He'd even admitted that modern Japan was evolving. "It's a different time. A different world now."

"I can't take that chance."

One relative tried to destroy the country, and another protected it. A crazy sense of balance? And a motive for murder.

"Information like this can't stay hidden forever," I said. "Too many people are searching for answers."

Michael's body language said otherwise. I swallowed hard. "When did you find out about Haruto?"

"When my father died and I inherited the key to the safety deposit box." His anguish hurt. He'd lost more than a strong patriarch that day. The weight of his family's honor had fallen on his shoulders.

Was the knowledge a curse or a gift? Paula's had been a handful.

"You've had the Douglas Diamond for a long time," I said. His flinch gave it away. I'd been right. "I know what you're

167

going through. The Douglas Diamond is haunting. You can't get it out of your mind. You see it everywhere. In the sunset. Even in the golden poppies. I know. I held the Shepard Diamond. Its power is alluring. You feel invincible."

My heart felt the words worked. Michael steepled his hands. "My son will know what to do. He is a better man than I."

"He's still human. Do you want your legacy to him to be the same shame you've lived with for so long—the shame that your father fought for retribution over a lie and the shame of an even bigger secret?"

I let that thought settle in before I added, "What I do know is that you have the power to change the world in your hands."

He didn't believe me. I hardly believed it myself. I'd promised not to tell, but I could advocate for Logan Roma's heritage. "There's a young man who has waited four generations for his chance to shape history. The Douglas Diamond will allow him to fulfill his destiny." Listen to me talking about fate.

Not even a waver in Michael's set jaw. I tried once more. "It's never too late to do the right thing." Now I sounded like Russ. Was I already starting to think like him?

Michael advanced like a nimble big cat. I stepped back, suddenly uneasy. He matched my retreat step for step until my back hit the mirror. My fight-or-flight instincts took over, but I was pinned.

Winston knew it too. He filled the space between Michael and me, growling like an attack-ready Pit Bull.

"I didn't kill Paula. She was alive when I left her," Michael insisted. "You must believe me."

I should've just assured him I did, but I couldn't. "You hit her on the forehead with her walking stick. She bled out."

His anguish seemed real. "She wouldn't let me call 911 or

take her to a hospital. You know how argumentative she could be."

I did. "Half of Barkview will testify to it, for sure," I agreed.

"I regret listening to her." He didn't really. I could tell. In a flash, his calmness evaporated. Had it always been a façade? "I can't let you tell this story."

"It's not mine to tell." I meant it. Seemed like I'd said that a lot lately. What kind of edgy reporter was I? The honorable kind that respected privacy, the kind that people trusted with their real stories—the kind that I wanted to be. Despite the situation, a crazy calmness settled over me. After all this time, I finally knew where I belonged—where I'd always belonged. "You can't hide this. Too many people know."

"I should have destroyed the diamond years ago. Without it, the rest can't be linked. I just need your silence." His hands went for my throat. A vision of Russ came to mind. I sucked in my breath. Ready...

Instinctively, I shifted into a defensive stance. All my training in this very room came back with absolute clarity. Classic student-facing-teacher scenario. Will would determine the winner, as well as a Corgi whose namesake had toppled a superior force with sheer tenacity.

I'm not exactly sure how Winston did it. With full Corgi momentum, he launched at Michael's knees, causing him to stagger. Then German Shepherd fur filled the void, flattening the karate master. I hadn't moved an inch when Uncle G and Russ arrived with handcuffs for the arrest.

CHAPTER 23

Paula's quest hadn't ended exactly as she'd planned, though Charles and the entire Smythe family added heroism to their remarkable history. In the end, revealing one family's secrets had unraveled another's. Was that the inherent price of closure?

I stood on my new home's backyard patio, admiring the golden glow haloing the red orange Santa Ana sunset over the Pacific Ocean, a real reminder that the Douglas Diamond had finally made its way home. Not into Logan Roma's uncle, the kingmaker's hands, much to his annoyance, but to the Douglas Trust, anonymously returned despite the staggering reward and with an adventure to rival the Shepard Diamond's to tell. That the Romas would one day get the stone's secrets, I had no doubt. Right now, I just felt relief that it was all over. Closure did matter.

Michael's fate would be decided by a jury of his peers. Had Paula's own stubbornness caused her death, or was it a simple case of murder? No one would know the real answer to that one.

Russ handed me a glass of shiraz du jour while Winston sat on my feet. No reason to displace him. Paula's granddaughter was on her way to pick him up. I'd miss his cute smile and quirky Corgi antics. The dog did relax me. I was even getting used to his herding tendencies and anticipated the tripping hazard. The constant shedding was definitely a deal breaker, though.

Russ draped his arm around me. "It's good to see you at peace."

I smiled. I was relaxed. I even had a plan for my role at KDOG that I'd discuss with Aunt Char in the next day or so. Not that she'd be surprised.

I raised my glass. The light filtering through the ruby liquid cast a shadowed symbol on the freshly laid travertine patio. I blinked twice. "It's a heart!"

Russ smiled. He saw it too. "Apropos."

The picture-perfect sky and the unexpected symbol of love all added up to the answer I'd been searching for. "Let's get married right here. This exact time tomorrow. Aunt Char can officiate. I'm sure we can find two witnesses." Before the winds changed and the enchantment became just another chapter in the Douglas Diamond's lore.

Russ's smile widened. As if he'd anticipated it all this time.

Our wedding came together with true Barkview spirit and Aunt Char's magical organizational skills twenty-four hours later. I stood just inside my home's French doors, admiring the rose-covered arch and the ocean backdrop. I was almost ready. Jennifer gave me the thumbs-up signal as she stood with a mouthful of hemming pins. She'd just completed alterations on Skye Barklay's magnificent Worth evening gown—the one she'd waltzed in with George V. Who knew, in addition to her many other skills, that Jennifer was a talented seamstress? Under the watchful eye of her two Cavaliers, she'd altered the dress perfectly. "It's your something-old." She hugged me. "You are beautiful."

Alicia and Misha the Fashionista breezed in with my something-new item. A pair of crystal-studded shoes that fit like they'd been made for me.

My sister, Lani, arrived next with a hatbox. "Madame Orr left this for you. She said she expects this to be returned to Dalsia in the spring."

No doubt guaranteeing my inclusion in upcoming events. I grinned. I couldn't help myself. What could she have possibly left for me? I pulled the blue ribbon. Atop black velvet sat a stunning antique diamond tiara. Lani's gasp mirrored mine.

I read the card aloud. "True love is not measured in gold. But diamonds always make it better."

"Geez. It's a princess's tiara, Cat. Look at the inscription. That's Queen Victoria's seal. What a something-borrowed," Lani said.

No kidding. Lani placed the tiara on my head while I preened in front of the mirror. It was heavier than I'd expected, but oh-so-blingalicious. I owed Madame Orr for this addition.

My mother entered a moment later, dressed in a three-quarter-length Hawaiian floral dress that matched my sister's. She presented me with my father's blue Distinguished Service Medal. "He'd be honored if you wore his blue."

And remembered all it represented. I bit back tears. Madame Orr had been right. My father's teachings would always be with me. "How did you get here so quickly?"

Mom smiled. "A general held a flight for me. Your husband has friends in high places."

Of course he did. Russ wouldn't let me get married without my mother in attendance. *Husband.* I liked the sound of it.

As I walked down the rose-petaled path between my mother and sister toward that meaningful sunset, I saw a

172

fleeting glimpse of the Shepard and Douglas Diamonds coming together in the sinking sun. This wasn't the end; it was the beginning. A single golden sun would rise in the morning, bringing new hope.

My gaze met Aunt Char's misty one beneath the rose arch. Her Cavalier King Charles, Renny, sat to her right and Winston, dressed in a tuxedo, to her left. Russ stood to her right with Uncle G and his German Shepherds beside him. Sandy and Jack waited to Aunt Char's left. Jack sat still, proudly showing off the rose boutonniere attached to his collar. Sandy held a yellow rose bouquet that matched mine.

Russ's mom and sister stood in the front row with her Portuguese water dog, Matata. My sorority sister, Rayelle, stood beside the Sit and Stay Café's owner, Nell, with their BFFs. Both women had whipped up a Michelin-worthy spread for later. Ariana, our jeweler, and her German Shepherd, Gem, stood beside Gabby and her Saluki. Will played the violin. Who knew our intrepid elevator operator played Bach like the man himself?

Champagne flowed as Aunt Char started the ceremony. The people that mattered to me most were all here as Russ and I stood in front of the magnificent sunset and said "I do" to a lifetime of adventures that we would figure out together.

The next morning the *Bark View's* front-page wedding photo missed the remarkable sky altogether. It didn't capture the attendees either. The picture featured Russ and me and ten dogs.

Barkview welcomed us to the family.

The End 🐾🐾🐾

I hope you enjoyed your adventure in the dog-friendliest place in America. To learn more about Barkview and Cat's next adventure, visit www.cbwilsonauthor.com.

Sign up for *The Bark View*, a monthly update on all things Barkview, including:

- *Friday Funnies*: pet-related cartoons
- *WOW*! A dog did that?
- Recipes from *Bichon Bisquets Barkery's* canine kitchen
- Cool merchandise ideas from the *Bow Wow Boutique*
- Not to mention Barkview news and fun contests.

Don't miss Cat's next adventure at Canine Cay, Australia, where the lore of fabled pearls turns a romantic honeymoon on the Great Barrier Reef into a race against time to catch a killer before Russ pays for the crime with his life.

COMING SOON: AUSSIED TO DEATH

What's not to love about an exotic honeymoon on a remote Australian island known for a legendary hidden treasure? Cat Wright is all in, until she arrives at Canine Cay and the Great Dingo Spirit speaks to her. Forget hunting for the treasure. Her new husband has been arrested for murder!

Convinced they have their man, the police aren't looking into other suspects. Cat knows it is up to her to clear Russ. Except the deeper she digs the guiltier he appears. And his link to the treasure is only the beginning...

Is this an elaborate frame or is Russ's past going to derail their marriage before it has a chance to begin? Can Cat and her Aussie companion locate the treasure and prove Russ's innocence before the real murderer buries her happily ever after forever?

ACKNOWLEDGMENTS

To my writing cheerleaders Pam Wright, Dee Kaler, Bill Hubiak, Becky Witters, Noel Mohberg and Brandi Wilson, who endlessly listen to my ideas, edit my spelling and grammar, help research and test recipes, thank you.

For research and police procedure assistance, thank you to Richard R. Zitzke, Chief of Police, Whitehall, Ohio, retired. I assure you any errors are entirely my fault.

Thank you Charisse Wolfe, Derby and Belmont. You all inspired Winston.

As always, Melissa Martin. You keep me sane.

ABOUT THE AUTHOR

C.B. Wilson's love of writing began after she read her first Nancy Drew book and reworked the ending. Studying at the Gemology Institute of America, she discovered a passion for researching lost, stolen, and missing diamonds. The big kind. Her fascination with dogs and their passionate owners inspired Barkview, California, the dog-friendliest city in America.

C.B. lives in Peoria, Arizona, with her husband. She is an avid pickleball player who enjoys traveling to play tournaments. She admits to chocoholic tendencies and laughing out loud at dog comics.

Connect with C.B. Wilson at: www.cbwilsonauthor.com
Facebook: www.facebook.com/cbwilsonauthor
Instagram: www.instagram.com/cbwilsonauthor

AUTHOR'S NOTE

As you have probably figured out, I love history. It inspires me to write the "what could've happened" every time. World War II California was no exception. Japanese submarines were sighted off the California coast in 1941-1942. The bombing of the Elwood refinery off Santa Barbara, California, did happen. (I thought only Pearl Harbor, Hawaii had been attacked.) Spies in California were also real. Could there have been spies operating off the Channel Islands? Why not?

Dogs did help patrol the California beaches during World War II. Dogs also carried battlefield messages during both World Wars. The Fish Creek Mountain earthquake did occur on October 21, 1942, in a remote inland area, but caused little damage to coastal San Diego.

Americans of Japanese descent were sent to internment camps on the mainland US. Hawaii was under martial law from December 7, 1941, to October 24, 1944. Station HYPO, or Fleet Radio Unit Pacific (FRUPAC), at Pearl Harbor was credited with breaking the Japanese JN-25 naval code which allowed a US victory at Midway. More than 10,000 women recruited from US colleges worked as code makers and breakers during World War II. Many were stationed at headquarters in Washington D.C. There is no official record of a woman serving at Station HYPO in Hawaii. If you have a chance, read *Code Girls: The Untold Story of the American Women Code Breakers of World War II* by Liza Mundy. The story inspires.

The "family" safety deposit boxes are a Barkview thing. Can you imagine what your grandparents would have stashed away for you?

Hope you enjoyed reading about Cat's adventures as much as I did writing about them. World War II has so many interesting stories to tell. Did you know that the Japanese almost invaded Australia? In 1942 they controlled territory just north of the country. So, get ready for an Aussie diamond hunt at Canine Cay, Australia, and "may the Great Dingo Spirit be with you and your BFF."

CPSIA information can be obtained
at www.ICGtesting.com
Printed in the USA
BVHW042038100423
662077BV00003B/39

9 798987 350317